newskids @n.the.net

NICK HANDEL

newskids @n.the.net

Matador
9 Priory Business Park
Kibworth Beauchamp
Leicestershire LE8 0RX, UK
Tel: (+44) 116 279 2299
Fax: (+44) 116 279 2277
Email: books@troubador.co.uk
Web: www.troubador.co.uk/matador

ISBN 978-1784620-028

British Library Cataloguing in Publication Data.
A catalogue record for this book is available from the British Library.

Typeset in Bembo by Troubador Publishing Ltd
Printed and bound in the UK by TJ International, Padstow, Cornwall

Matador is an imprint of Troubador Publishing Ltd

MIX
Paper from responsible sources
FSC® C013056
FSC www.fsc.org

newskids @n.the.net

Ever wondered what it would be like to have your own TV station? With the help of two best mates, fourteen-year-old Max Taylor finds a way to create one in his dad's garden shed; but when a girl at school goes missing, Newskids on the Net becomes the nerve centre of a desperate nationwide search. Soon, the kids themselves are front page news and propelled into a deadly adventure where kidnaps, late night stake-outs and secret recordings lead to a nerve-jangling climax at a World Cup semifinal at Wembley Stadium.

All characters in the story are fictitious, but the technology used by the Newskids to make their TV programmes is part of most children's everyday lives. While I was writing the book, the kids' way of webcasting seemed ahead of its time; but now there is no limit to the excitement and innovation resourceful young minds can bring to our screens.

Nick Handel.

NICK HANDEL

Nick Handel is a former BBC producer whose many credits include Children in Need (with Terry Wogan and Sue Cook), 'In at the Deep End' (with Chris Serle and Paul Heiney), 'Jobs For The Girls' (with Pauline Quirke and Linda Robson), The Search (with Nick Ross and Fiona Bruce) and The Teaching Awards. He began his career in local radio where, beside coping with the pressures of daily journalism and producing live topical magazine programmes, he wrote and presented scores of children`s short stories. Moving to Television in 1976, he became film director on That`s Life! making stars of Tramp, an Old English sheepdog who drove a car and Prince, a talking Yorkshire Terrier who made the world "Sausages!" a national catchphrase. Nick is a highly acclaimed documentary-maker, with a strong reputation for storytelling. Now freelance, he spends much of his time passing on his experience to the next generation of producers and directors. He also works extensively in schools using film techniques to stimulate creative writing skills. His concepts have now been published in an educational resource for teachers called "Calling the Shots!" (Pogo Learning). The package, which is fully illustrated, includes a DVD of mini-dramas for children to translate from screen to page. There is also a section on how to tell great stories on video using ordinary domestic equipment.

www.newskidsonthenet.co.uk
www.pogolearning.com

For Carolyn, Tim, Mickie and Ted

CONTENTS

Chapter 1

THREE KIDS, THE GOSS AND AN ANGRY CAT

Sniffer was in a hurry. It was January 15th, his fourteenth birthday, but he was trying to ignore the thoughts of unopened presents that danced enticingly through his freckled red head. First, there was a deadline to meet and his tubby legs whirled like Catherine wheels as they powered a battered old bike along a pitch dark, frosty lane.

Ollie 'Sniffer' Morris was the photographer of The Goss, a weekly newsletter he helped produce with his friends Max and Becky who had nicknamed him 'Sniffer' because he could smell a great news story from five miles away. With a circulation of two hundred and fifty, The Goss was no threat to The Sun or The Daily Mail; but the neighbours in Goss Street looked forward to catching up with all the local chit-chat when free copies arrived by e-mail every Wednesday at seven o'clock sharp.

Today was Wednesday. It was already five thirty and The Goss went to press at six. Suddenly, Ollie's hip pocket began to vibrate and an American police siren wailed through the freezing night air. He swerved, pulling his mobile phone from the tangle of pencils, rubber bands and Snickers wrappers that clogged the pockets of his new jeans.

"Ollie Morris!" he panted, steering unsteadily with one hand.

"What's happening, Sniff?" barked a voice. "You're late!"

Ollie had a sinking feeling in the pit of his stomach. It was Max Taylor, his editor,and it was clear that this was no social call.

"Where's that amazing picture story you promised us for page two?"

The boys had been best friends for as long as they could remember, but Max could be very demanding on press days and, like all good press photographers, Ollie was a master at talking his way out of tight corners.

"I'm minutes away," he lied, piling on the speed. "You're going to love it when you see my shots. Gotta go. Laters!"

The depressing truth was that Sniffer Morris didn't *have* an amazing picture story for page two. Pocketing the mobile, he was trying to dream up some plausible excuse when a black cat darted out of the darkness and froze in the beam of his cycle lamp.

"Get out of the waaaaaaaay!" he yelled, hitting a sheet of black ice that sent him careering into the kerb and flying over the handlebars into a tall bush. Slowly and painfully, he pulled himself from its thorny branches and glanced back at the bike. It was lying at the roadside, its front wheel ticking quietly as it spun over a motionless black moggie.

"Oh, my God, I've killed it!" he panicked, rubbing his knee through a rip in his jeans. As he stumbled over to the wreckage, a bad-tempered hiss reassured him that the creature had survived. Sighing with relief, he took his camera from the saddlebag and took a shot through the revolving spokes, then continued his journey – steering slightly left to compensate for a seriously wonky front wheel.

The atmosphere in Max Taylor's bedroom was buzzing as stories for The Goss took shape. Handouts from dozens of local organisations and clubs were scattered across the duvet or stuck to the wall alongside his photograph collection of TV newsreaders. Pride of place was given to the BBC's Greg Armstrong and the young editor could hardly wait for a date to be announced for a talk the star had promised to give at school later that term.

The Taylors had moved to Goston just before Max was born. His father, Nick,made TV commercials and his mother, Sue, taught at the local primary school. They were a popular couple whose pride and joy was a long, unruly garden in which Mr.Taylor had spent most of the summer building a huge, rickety shed. He was now working from home on a big new campaign idea and, as Ollie's bike limped into Goss Street, Max was rushing downstairs to his study, closely followed by Becky Roberts who was in charge of layout for The Goss.

"It's quarter to six, dad!" he shouted, shouldering his way in clutching handfuls of notes. "May we come in now?"

Mr. Taylor was used to being evicted every

Wednesday so that The Goss team could put the finishing touches to their paper on the Adman Eye-Power Plus P.C., but today he had a deadline of his own to meet – and things weren't going well.

"Blast!" he groaned. "I've got to make a really important presentation in the morning and it's just eaten my storyboards! I *hate* this machine!"

"No worries!" said Becky, who knew that Mr. Taylor's computer skills were on a par with the average orang-utan's. "I'll soon have you sorted!"

Small and feisty with a pretty, sensitive face, Becky was in the same class as Max and Ollie at Bridgemont School in Goston. She lived with her mum in a neat little cottage off the High Street and had a slight stammer which could be really annoying for her – especially when she was under pressure. French orals were a complete nightmare, but there was no-one to touch her when it came to I.T. Max and Ollie liked to call her their 'IT Girl', a pet name she pretended to hate, but which secretly made her feel special and quite proud.

"This won't take a mo," she said brightly, her fingers flying across the keyboard until Mr. Taylor's work reappeared. "Don't forget to hit 'save' next time."

"You're a star, Becky," said Max's long-suffering dad, heading for the kitchen to watch the news. He was resigned to the household being disrupted by his son's obsession with newspapers, but sometimes wished he would get another life: football, skate-boarding, bungee-jumping – perhaps even a girlfriend. Becky shared that thought. Her feelings for Max were becoming more grown-up, but she worried that he saw her only as a computer nerd and wished she were better at being cool and sophisticated.

Suddenly, the door crashed open and Ollie flew in, baseball cap askew and sweatshirt hanging out of his ripped jeans. He traded high fives with Max and flung himself onto a beanbag with a blood-curdling yell.

"Quiet, Sniff!" shouted Becky, who was trying to finish the entertainment section. "It's ten to six. You've made me lose my p..p..place!"

"Sor-ry!" said Ollie indignantly. "Don't I even get a 'Sniff, you're a legend for schlepping all over Goston in the freezing cold looking for amazing picture stories'?"

She raised her eyebrows as he handed her his camera and turned to Max.

"Have you got any Dr Pepper, mate?" he asked, ripping his way into a packet of M & Ms. "I'm dying of thirst here."

Photography and good living ran in Ollie's family. His father, Trevor, owned a camera shop called Say Cheese and his mother, Eileen, ran the local Weight Watchers club. Ollie disapproved of this because he was proud of being a rounder person and saw absolutely no reason why anyone should want to be slim.

"Just chill for a minute, Sniff," said Max, waiting eagerly for Becky to upload the pictures. "You can have a whole bucketful of Dr Pepper if these shots are any good."

"Ta-Daaaah!" trumpeted Becky as a solitary image appeared on the screen. "The moment we've all been kept waiting for!"

Then her voice trailed off and Max's jaw dropped like a stone.

"What's this?" he asked, sweeping the floppy blond fringe out of his eyes and nudging his gold-rimmed glasses up onto his forehead. "We've been holding half a page for this 'amazing picture story' – and you come back with one shot of a rubbishy old cat under a bike. What's so amazing about that?"

Ollie was searching his brain for an explanation, but couldn't find one.

"Maybe there's something you haven't told us," Max continued sarcastically. "Like it's a member of a four-legged sprint cycling team – or does it mend punctures instead of eating mice…?"

The tubby photographer was getting more and more uncomfortable, but his friend wouldn't let it drop.

"… Perhaps it eats bicycles! Now, that *would* be a great story…!"

That was the last straw. Ollie had wrecked his bike, ripped his jeans and was in no mood for being humiliated by smart-alec newspaper editors – even if this one was his best mate.

"It happens to be my birthday, in case you've forgotten!" he exploded. "I've been freezing my butt off for two hours looking for your picture story and the most amazing thing I could find was a bloke arguing over the price of a tin of beans in Sainsbury's. What did you expect me to do – start a fire at the church hall?"

Becky was used to being the calming influence when things got tense. Both she and Ollie respected

Max and knew that The Goss couldn't survive without his leadership and ideas; but he could be headstrong and sometimes needed cutting down to size when he was in one of his bossy moods.

"Lighten up, guys," she said. "Animal Safety Week's coming up. Maybe Sniff's picture could be a reminder to look out for pets near busy roads."

Max's mood lifted and he began to scribble headline ideas into a notebook.

"Great idea, Becky!" he murmured, nibbling thoughtfully at a pen as he scanned the list and chose his favourite. "We'll call it *'THE CAT THAT 'SPOKE' UP FOR ROAD SAFETY.'*" Then he smiled at Ollie. "I was out of order there, Sniff. Sorry I gave you a hard time. Happy birthday!"

Ollie's face lit up as Max presented him with a box of freshly-baked choc-chip cookies.

"Sweet!" he said, offering them round. "Cheers, bro. Perhaps you have your good points after all!"

The tension evaporated and the trio returned to the task in hand. Max, Becky and Ollie were only children and their relationship had grown more akin to brothers and sister, weathering spats and fallings-out as though they were part and parcel of ordinary family life.

"Anything for the sports section, Sniff?" asked Becky, holding her cookie between her teeth as she pounded the keyboard. "We're nearly out of time."

Ollie beamed as he pulled a crumpled score sheet from his back pocket. If there was one thing he loved more than chocolate it was football and he'd be in seventh heaven come the summer when England was hosting the World Cup.

"Goss Street Under 15s lost five nil to Chalcroft," he smirked, knowing the defeat would be one in the eye for the Goss Street coach who had excluded him from team trials for being unfit and overweight. He was about to say something very rude when Max cut in.

"Do we have anything from Neighbourhood Watch?" he asked, switching back into 'editor' mode as he spotted an empty space in the middle of page one.

"Oh, I f..forgot," cried Becky, riffling through a mountain of press releases. "They want us to put out a warning about some lowlife creep who talks his way into old peoples' houses by pretending to be a gas man. He stole a hundred quid from Mrs. Williams last week and she's given the police a really g..good description. He's tall with a dark, droopy moustache and brown horn-rimmed glasses."

"Shame we haven't got one of those photofits," mused Ollie. "That would fill the space really well."

"Who needs a photofit?" exclaimed Max, having one of his brainwaves. "My dad's got glasses like that – *and* he's tall and dark. All he needs is a false moustache and you can take a shot. It'll be just like one of those reconstructions on "Crimewatch"!"

"You've got a nerve, Max Taylor!" chided Becky. "The things you do to your poor father!"

"He'll be fine," chuckled Max. "So long as it jogs a few memories and helps catch the crook. Come on! Time to get creative with mum's eyeliner."

"I heard that!" said a suspicious Mr. Taylor, entering the room to collect his brief case. "What's all this about "Crimewatch" and mum's eyeliner?"

It wouldn't be the first time he had fallen victim to his son's big ideas and some of the memories were still raw. He often had nightmares about the time he was strapped to a board at the local circus while Ollie snapped a huge, bare-chested Hungarian knife-thrower planting razor-sharp blades inches from his head; but before he could protest, Becky had drawn something resembling a black, furry caterpillar over his upper lip and he found himself facing the camera.

"Try to look sly, Mr. T!" directed Ollie, framing Max's father in the front doorway just as his mum arrived back from a parents' meeting.

"You're as bad as the kids!" she scoffed, raising her eyebrows as she squeezed past her husband who was narrowing his eyes like a pantomime villain. Mr. Taylor held the expression, trying to convince himself that anything was worthwhile if it protected defenceless old people from predatory con men with unsightly facial hair; then Ollie pressed the shutter. Moments later, Becky had set the picture into the page under another of Max's dramatic headlines: *'IF A MOUSTACHE LIKE THIS KNOCKS AT YOUR DOOR, DON'T LET IT IN!'*

"Right, guys!" he cried, scrolling through the completed paper. "One quick spell-check and off she goes!"

At two minutes past seven, edition 24 of The Goss was e-mailed to every house in the street and it was time for Becky and Ollie to make their way home to the less newsworthy activities of homework, supper and evening TV.

"Night mum! Night dad!" said Max, heading for

bed as the closing headlines of the Ten O'Clock News faded from the screen. Before long, he was snuggled under his duvet watching the full moon floating across a black, cloudless sky as though it, too, were searching for stories. A pallid glow dappled the forest of papers that covered his bedroom walls, catching the photograph of Greg Armstrong. He closed his eyes, holding the thought that came to him every night before he fell asleep: "I'm going to be a newsman – one day!"

Chapter 2

MIDNIGHT NEWSROOM

"You've shaved it off!" shouted a muscular woman in curlers and a wrap-around apron as Mr. Taylor sprinted into Station Road at eight o'clock next morning. He had to be on time for his presentation and couldn't afford to miss the train; but she flung herself in front of him, blocking his path and shrieking to her husband at the top of her voice: "Quick, George! It's that conniving gas man out of The Goss. The ugly brute has shaved off that big 'airy moustache, but he don't fool me!"

A small crowd began to gather as a beefy, unshaven man came lumbering out of the house clutching a baseball bat and a copy of The Daily Mirror. Mr. Taylor tried to protest, but received a sharp dig in the midriff with the rolled-up newspaper. He decided to keep quiet. One more word and it could have been a whack with the baseball bat.

"I'll have Max boiled in oil for this!" he hissed through clenched teeth as the train pulled in to the station. "He deserves to be grounded for a week!"

Doors slammed and the 8.03 rumbled on its way, leaving him stranded and struggling to explain.

Max and Becky arrived at school to the usual Thursday chorus of "Don't believe everything you read in the papers!" but it always gave them a buzz when The Goss got a reaction. Ollie had missed the bus – and not for the first time. The staff were used to him flying into assembly at the last minute, charming them with one of his original and highly improbable excuses; but it would take more than charm to handle the trouble lurking behind the cycle sheds that morning: Keith Pratt and Jason Steed had him in their sights.

Pratt was the school bully – and revelled in the distinction. He was almost six feet tall and built like the side of a house. His greasy hair, spotty complexion and dark, piggy eyes gave him the appearance of an overcooked pizza and he did a roaring trade taking sweets and small change from the smaller kids in return for protecting them from what he called 'unfortunate little slaps'. His sidekick was Jason Steed, a thin, weedy fourteen-year-old whose only other friend in the world was an older sister, Josie, who was in the year above. Jason was terrified of Keith who took pleasure in forcing him to do everything he asked.

"How sad are you, fatty?" sneered Pratt as Ollie came bounding into school, still doing up his tie and munching a piece of dry toast. "Haven't you got anything better to do than sit up all night writing naff newspapers? Why don't you weirdos get a life?"

Ollie hated being called 'fatty', but ignored the insult and kept walking towards the hall until Keith grabbed him from behind and slammed him hard into the corrugated iron shed. The tubby teenager was renowned for shouting like a ship's fog horn and his distress call brought Max and Becky racing to the scene.

"Leave him alone, you c..c…creeps!" shouted Becky, seeing a painful red mark appearing under her friend's left eye.

"Shut it, stutterer!", snarled Pratt, tightening his grip on Ollie's collar. "Tell you what. As I'm in a generous mood, I'll make you a deal. If you can say 'Leave him alone, you creeps' like a *normal* person, I'll let fat boy go…"

"Ow!!!!" gasped Ollie as Pratt squeezed his throat even harder, making him choke.

"L…L..Leave…him.." stammered Becky, making a huge effort to protect her friend; but Keith Pratt only sniggered.

"Is that the best you can do?" he sneered. "Why don't you learn to talk properly like everybody else?"

"L..leave him alone you c..c…" she struggled; but the harder she tried, the more the stammer gripped her until tears began to well in her eyes and her neck broke out in blotches. By now, Ollie had turned red in the face and Max knew that somehow he'd have to make this walking mountain let go – even though he was half Keith's size.

"Quick! Aynsley's coming!" he shouted, elbowing the lout hard in the stomach and yanking him back by his greasy mullet. Pratt wasn't the brightest kid in the school, but knew that the headmaster came down hard on bullying. Without a sideways glance, he dropped

Ollie like a hot potato and legged it to the safety of the hall leaving Jason to take the blame as usual; but before either realised that Max had tricked them, Ollie was safe.

"Thanks, dude!" he croaked, straightening his tie and pretending the attack had been no big deal. "I could have bought them off with a couple of Yorkie bars, but what's the point of wasting good chocolate on a pair of losers like that?"

"They'll get what they deserve one day," said Becky, giving him a comforting hug. "Sorry I let you down, Sniff. Come on or we'll miss assembly."

Derek Aynsley, M.A., was a stout, red-faced man with heavy jowls and a number of warts standing out on his forehead and cheeks. Bristling black eyebrows meeting in the middle gave him a severe, combative air that belied a gentle nature and a very strong sense of fair play.

"There are still tickets left for our school play, 'Midnight Newsroom'," he was saying as they slid quietly in at the back of the hall. "Mr. Bradley tells me that Rachael Cooper is showing great promise in the leading role and I hope that everyone will support her, and the rest of the cast, by filling the hall next Friday and Saturday when performances begin at seven thirty..."

"Who's this Rachael Cooper?" whispered Ollie, who was immediately 'shushed' by Mrs. Farthing who was sitting at the end of their row.

"...And finally, a special date for your diaries," concluded the Head, peering over his silver half-moon spectacles. "I'm delighted to say that Greg Armstrong, the BBC Television foreign correspondent and newsreader, has confirmed that he will speak to us after school next Tuesday. This promises to be a very popular event and will be open to pupils and parents on a first come, first served basis. It is now nine fifteen, so please proceed quickly and quietly to your first lessons."

There was only one thought on Max's mind as he raced down the back staircase: how could he get a personal interview with Greg Armstrong for The Goss? Without looking where he was going, he hurtled into the corridor leading to Mr. Sanderson's Geography room and collided head-on with a tall, very beautiful girl with long blond hair styled in a mass of curls. The large cardboard box she was carrying flew into the air, but she managed to catch it just before it hit the floor, striking a pose like a dancer at the end of a big routine.

"I can't believe I did that!" apologised Max as they stooped to gather their scattered books. "Are you O.K.?"

"It was a bit of a shock," said the girl, who spoke with an American accent. "But I guess I'll live!"

Max had seen her around at school, but didn't know who she was. Her whole demeanour was larger than life and her fun-filled eyes sparkled with personality. He tried to think of something witty to say but, for once, his tongue was tied in knots.

"Trade you Masterson's Guide to the South American Rain Forests for my 'Midnight Newsroom' script and we're even!" she said, playfully passing him the atlas he had dropped in the collision. "My name's Rachael Cooper."

"Rachael Cooper!" gushed Max, feeling slightly uncool as he took the book and gave her hand an enthusiastic shake. "You're the actress. Mr. Aynsley talked about you in assembly."

"Guilty as charged!" she giggled, retrieving her arm. "My mom and dad moved here from Boston last fall. This is my first term at Bridgemont. I'm in year ten. It's good to know you."

Suddenly, Max felt his news reporter's curiosity kicking in.

"Max Taylor, year nine," he said. "What's in the box?"

"Oh, that's my costume," she replied, raising a corner of the lid and sliding the script inside. "We're having a dress rehearsal in the hall this afternoon. Everything's gotten kind of scary with just a week to go and it's a nightmare remembering all the words. Still, it'll be alright on the night, I guess!"

As she moved away, Max gave a gentle cough. He wanted to leave a better impression than being a clumsy geek with an embarrassing handshake and a disastrous line in chat.

"I run a local paper with some mates," he added matter-of-factly. "Suppose I bring my photographer along to your rehearsal? We could run a preview piece next Wednesday. It might sell a few extra tickets."

The idea of publicity clearly appealed and Rachael quickly turned back.

"Sounds great!" she said, eyeing him with renewed interest. "I'll be sure and do my hair and make-up. The rehearsal starts at four thirty. Don't be late, now!"

The day ended with double I.T. which was a

highlight of the timetable because Max, Becky and Ollie were in the same group and Charles Dudgeon, who had the very grand title of Head of Information and Communication Technology, was the most popular, if worst dressed, teacher in the school. They were designing a website to raise awarenessof Goston's natural environment and Becky was enjoying her role as project manager. She hardly stammered in the I.T. room and, although having Jason Steed in the group made life unduly stressful at times, Mr. Dudgeon had an infallible method of nipping the slightest hint of trouble in the bud: it was a webcam mounted just above the whiteboard which acted as his second pair of eyes.

Charles Dudgeon dashed into the classroom looking flustered and extremely hot in a shapeless green jumper with a faded orange buffalo knitted across the chest.

"I've just come from a meeting with the Head," he puffed, rummaging for his glasses in the pockets of a baggy pair of corduroy trousers. "He wants the site up and running by tonight. There's a school inspection tomorrow and we *must* be on line."

A murmur of apprehension ran through the group and all eyes turned to Becky.

"No pressure, guys!" she joked, determined not to let her stammer betray the doubts that were gathering in her mind. "Can I have your piece on grey squirrels please,Katy? And I'll need a picture of Mr. Aynsley, Sniff – to go with the introduction he's written for the home p..page."

"No probs," said Ollie grabbing his camera case.

"I'll go to his office straight away. Anything else need shooting while I'm at it?"

Becky shot a meaningful glance at Jason, but decided to say nothing as she sent Ollie on his way and walked over to Max who was keen to show her something on his P.C.

"Wait till you see this!" he chuckled. "I've just downloaded it from the internet."

"Yuk!" she gasped as a hideous toad's head appeared on the screen – a grotesque leathery blob of warts with huge bulging eyes. Without pausing for breath, Max broke into a dreadful impersonation of Sir David Attenborough:

"When mating, males croak continuously to attract females," he read in an earnest whisper. "They will stop at nothing, including crossing busy roads, to reach spawning sites. Help a toad across the road and lower the death toll in *your* area. Join a toad patrol – now!"

"Wicked!" laughed Becky, suddenly feeling much more confident. "It sets up the conservation angle brilliantly and the picture's great."

Soon the room was alive with activity, but although the group worked hard over the next two hours, there was still a long way to go when the bell rang for end of school.

"P..please can I stay on for a while, Mr. Dudgeon?" pleaded Becky, determined not to be beaten and completely unfazed as her classmates streamed out of the room. "Another hour should do it – and I'm sure Max and Ollie will help me out."

"Only if you promise to take the key back to the caretaker's office," requested her teacher, zipping up a fluorescent jacket and fastening his cycle clips. "I'd like to stay with you, but I don't think my daughter would ever forgive me. It's her birthday, you see, and we're celebrating at McDonalds. Good luck – and don't stay too late, will you?"

A freezing draught blew in as he left the room wearing a pair of elasticated goggles that made him look more like a polar explorer than a schoolmaster on a quest for cheeseburgers and fries.

The three friends were soon so engrossed in their task that they lost all track of time until Max glanced at his watch and clapped both hands to the sides of his head.

"Oh no!" he groaned. "Rachael Cooper…I forgot Rachael Cooper!"

"Who's Rachael Cooper?" asked Becky who was struggling to finish the final page.

"She's starring in the school play," Max reminded her, sounding quite agitated as he tugged Ollie towards the door. "I promised that Sniff and I would cover her dress rehearsal at half past four and it's after six! Can you manage here, Becky? If we don't go straight to the hall, it will all be over and she'll think I'm full of hot air."

Becky didn't really care what Rachael Cooper thought. The pressure was getting to her and, at that moment, life seemed very unfair. She'd been abandoned by her teacher,deserted by her classmates and now her two best friends were off to give the V.I.P. treatment to a jumped-up little actress she didn't even know.

"Go if it's that important," she flounced with a

meaningful sigh. "I'll drop the key back – but this Rachael Cooper story had b..b..better be worth it, that's all I can say!"

As they entered the hall, Max and Ollie were amazed at the scale of Mr. Bradley's production. 'Midnight Newsroom' was set in an American TV station and the stage had been transformed into a studio with four very realistic cameras made out of cardboard boxes. Rachael fitted the part of anchor-woman Penny Rassin to a tee. She was only a year above them, but looked nearer twenty-five than fifteen in an elegant designer suit with sharp lapels and a waisted jacket.

"Good evening, and welcome to the Midnight Newsroom," she was saying as a red light glowed on top of camera one. "The headlines at one a.m…."

Ollie snapped a Crunchie bar in two and offered half to Max who was too busy staring at Rachael to even notice.

"Like older women, do you?" he teased, bringing his pal down to earth with a bump.

"Don't be a jerk!" huffed Max, reddening with embarrassment. "That girl's a natural TV presenter. It sounds as if she's been reading the news all her life."

Ollie enjoyed getting Max rattled, but before he could wind him up again the rehearsal ended and it was time to get their story.

"Must you take pictures *now*?" asked Mr. Bradley who was keen to get away for the evening.

"There's no such thing as bad publicity, sir," Ollie pointed out, adding with an innocent grin: "And didn't the Head say something about wanting to fill the hall on both nights…?"

Mr. Bradley was left with no choice.

"You could sell snowballs to an Eskimo, Ollie Morris!" he smiled, shaking his head as he turned to a small, dishevelled technician with holes in his jumper and a pair of headphones hanging round his neck. "Look after them, will you Sparks? I'll be back to lock up in ten minutes."

Akbar Khan was known as 'Sparks' because he was a genius with electronics – especially lighting and sound. He threw some switches on the console and the words 'Midnight Newsroom' blazed onto the scenery behind the news desk where Rachael was carefully checking her hair and make-up.

"You look wicked, Rachael!" chirped Ollie, framing her in his viewfinder with the air of a fashion photographer on the catwalks of Milan. "I'm Ollie Morris. I'll get some nice natural shots while Max does the interview, but don't forget to look at me from time to time. I'm the good-looking one, remember!"

Rachael tossed back her mane of blond hair and let out a peal of infectious, if slightly theatrical, laughter.

"Did you do any research for the part?" asked Max, feeling more confident as he opened his notebook and took control.

"Oh, for sure!" exclaimed Rachael, as though she were playing to a full house. "I guess I've been researching it most of my life. A television presenter is the only thing I've ever wanted to be. Landing a job in news would be a dream come true for me."

Max's eyes lit up.

"How weird is that?" he gasped as Ollie snapped away in the background. "I want to be a newsman, too

– but I'd be happier working behind the cameras than in front. Are you going to Greg Armstrong's lecture next Tuesday?"

"Just try and stop me!"

There was a pause. He thought about asking her to go with him, but the words wouldn't come and, by the time Mr. Bradley returned with the keys, the moment had passed.

"Great interview, Max!" called Rachael, flinging her school uniform into the cardboard box and flying out of the hall to meet her mother who was very proud that her daughter was becoming such a hit in her very first year at Bridgemont.

Sue Taylor was *anything* but proud when Max arrived home from school over two hours late. She was tired after a stressful day's teaching and angry that he hadn't bothered to ring.

"What's the matter, mum?" he asked, sensing that something was wrong.

"That newspaper of yours is what's the matter!" she snapped, lifting a charred pizza out of the oven. "Someone mistook dad for that con man this morning and made a citizen's arrest. If the police hadn't turned up, he might have been lynched."

Max knew that, under normal circumstances, his mother would have seen the funny side of her husband's innocent brush with the law, but this time things had clearly got out of hand.

"He missed his presentation, Max," she sighed. "The agency almost lost the account he's been working on and he could have got the sack. Look, we both know how much The Goss means to you – and you'll always have our support. But you mustn't let it take over your life. Family and school are important, too. If you want to run a newspaper, I'm sure your time will come – but it won't happen if everything else takes a back seat. Now eat your supper and get on with your homework. Dad will be home in an hour – and there are some fences to mend."

Chapter 3

A TASTE OF THE BIG TIME

The atmosphere was frosty in the Taylor household that night, but it was positively arctic next morning on the school bus.

"How fit is Rachael Cooper?" drooled Ollie with all the tact of a charging rhinoceros. "Why aren't you taking her to Greg's lecture on Tuesday? You were almost in there – and you blew it!"

Max gave him a sharp kick on the ankle, but it was too late.

"I may not be as fit as Rachael Cooper," said Becky, sounding wretched and unloved. "But it would be nice if s..someone asked how *I* got on last night."

Max was devastated to see her so upset and felt thoroughly ashamed of himself.

"I'm sorry, Becky," he said. "I'm not thinking straight. That gas man stunt almost got dad fired and he gave me a really hard time last night. I hope you didn't have to stay too late."

"I just about finished," she said flatly, avoiding eye contact and staring gloomily out of the window. "But I'd have missed the six thirty bus if it hadn't been for

Jason Steed.Mr. Robinson saw him coming out of detention and made him take the key back for me."

There was an awkward silence until the coach pulled into Bridgemont School and everyone piled out into the playground. As they walked towards the hall, Max was trying to think how to make things up to Becky when Mrs. Parsons, the headmaster's secretary, grabbed him roughly by the shoulder.

"You're in big trouble, Max Taylor," she hissed, frogmarching him to the Head's office where Derek Aynsley was waiting at his desk, incandescent with rage.

"You wanted to see me, sir?" said Max feeling bewildered and scared as Mrs.Parsons left the room. Without a word, Mr. Aynsley turned to his P.C. and clicked on the Environment Awareness site, swivelling the screen towards the ashen-faced schoolboy. Max watched in silence as the home page appeared, then shock waves coursed through his body. Ollie's photograph of the headmaster had vanished. In its place was the hideous, warted toad's head which was now wearing Mr. Aynsley's eyes, glasses, nose and mouth as it leered over a caption reading:

THE FAT, SPOTTED, RED-FACED
BRIDGEMONT TOAD
by MAX TAYLOR.

Flatten this monster before it's too late!
Join a toad patrol NOW!

"How dare you!" thundered the Head. "If this was your idea of a joke, it has failed miserably. If it was intended to humiliate me in front of the school inspectors, it has succeeded a hundred per cent and I think I'm entitled to an explanation!"

Max's blood had turned to ice. This was like being tried for a murder he hadn't committed and he had only seconds to come up with a case for the defence.

"W..with respect, sir," he protested, his stomach in knots of panic and confusion. "This has nothing to do with me. I found the picture on a conservation website, but I certainly didn't try to change it into you...I don't think you look anything like a toad, sir..."

"Silence!" roared the Head. "I will not tolerate this sort of puerile behaviour. You will take a two-hour detention after school next Tuesday – perhaps that will buck your ideas up a bit."

These words stung hardest of all and Max's legs buckled as he felt his world starting to collapse.

"But I c..can't!" he blurted, "Not on Tuesday...I'll miss Greg Armstrong's lecture! Oh, please don't make me do that, sir! Give me a four-hour detention any other day...I'll even come in at the weekend...but, I beg you, *please* not on Tuesday..."

But the headmaster was unmoved and it was a dazed and dejected Max who finally stumbled out onto the landing where Becky and Ollie were waiting to pick up the pieces.

"What did you do?" asked Ollie, trying to raise his spirits. "Strangle old Aynsley's Yorkshire terrier?"

"I know who I'd like to strangle," muttered Max who was still in shock as they made their way to the I.T. room. "I reckon Jason Steed did more than take the key back last night, Becky. I'll bet any money you like that he and Keith Pratt let themselves into Dudgeon's room and doctored the site."

Becky was furious when she saw what had happened.

"There's no way you can t..take the blame for this, Max," she fumed. "If it was down to Keith and Jason, we must report them!"

"But how do we prove it?" asked Ollie.

Max's keen brain was already working on that one, but first the damage had to be repaired and Becky was busily replacing the spoilt page when something caught her eye.

"Hang on a minute," she murmured, staring at the red light on Mr. Dudgeon's webcam glowing like a tiny beacon over the whiteboard. "There's a chance we may already *have* our proof. Keep a look out, will you, Sniff?"

Ollie peeped out into the corridor and gave the thumbs up that the coast was clear; then Becky went to work.

"What are you *doing*?" cried Max, his eyes widening in horror as she took control of Mr. Dudgeon's keyboard and mouse.

"I'm going into Dudgeon's hard drive," she said, pursing her lips. "He was in such a hurry to get away last night that he didn't close down his system."

"But that's *private*!" squeaked Max, quickly lowering his voice to a hoarse whisper. "I'm in enough trouble already without you making things worse!"

"Do you want to go to Greg Armstrong's lecture or not?" she hissed, completely undeterred. "If my hunch is right, the webcam records onto this media file – probably only a few frames a second, but that would be enough to identify our hackers."

The next click of the mouse brought up a bird's eye view of the I.T. room and Max's pulse raced as Becky sped through a recording of all yesterday's groups coming and going from their lessons until only she remained. The time code read 6.20.

"Don't think much of the movie!" joked Ollie, coming back to find out what was going on; but Max was in no mood for wisecracks. His eyes were glued to the screen watching Becky finishing work, packing up her things and turning out the lights; then the picture went dark – but the clock kept running. He held his breath, praying the machine wouldn't stop recording; but, to his relief, at exactly 6.35 the classroom light came on again and two figures skulked into the room, growing larger and larger as they moved towards her P.C.

"Gotcha!" cried Becky, grinning in triumph as she froze the frame. There was no doubting it now: the figures were Keith Pratt and Jason Steed, caught right in the act of defacing the site.

Suddenly, they almost jumped out of their skins as a deep voice rang out from the back of the room.

"I know you're in a spot of bother, Max Taylor, but don't you think it's just a tad out of order to be going through my computer files?"

Spinning round, Max sighed with relief as he saw the ample frame of Charles Dudgeon. It was as though a knight in shining armour had entered the room – but instead of a breastplate and plume, this one was wearing an old Status Quo sweatshirt and carrying a cycle helmet.

"Sorry, sir, but I was desperate!" he apologised.

"Becky noticed that you'd left your P.C. on overnight and we wondered if the real hackers had been picked up by the webcam."

"And...?"

"See for yourself." replied Becky, replaying the evidence.

Mr. Dudgeon watched the recording in silence, then left the room. Max glanced out of the window and saw him striding purposefully towards Mr. Aynsley's office. Suddenly, he knew he had a champion and something told him that everything would be alright.

★★★

"I apologise unreservedly for my hastiness this morning," said the headmaster when Max visited his study for the second time that day. "That act of mindless vandalism was a slap in the face to everyone who contributed to the website's success – but it doesn't excuse my putting two and two together and making five." He smiled and offered his hand. "I hope there are no hard feelings."

"No hard feelings, sir!" said Max, shaking it firmly. The rain clouds had lifted and he felt on top of the world again, but the Head hadn't finished.

"There is one further matter, however..."

Max froze, but the twinkle in Mr. Aynsley's eyes reassured him.

"...I've just spoken to Greg Armstrong at the BBC. I wondered if you might like to interview him for that newspaper of yours. He said he'd be happy to stay on for an extra half hour on Tuesday – provided that's alright with you, of course…"

Max had to pinch himself to make sure he wasn't dreaming. "ALRIGHT?" he said,"It's BETTER than alright. It's better than BRILLIANT!!! Wait till I tell Ollie and Becky. Thanks, Mr. Aynsley – you're a LEGEND!!!!"

★★★

At three forty-five the following Tuesday afternoon, a chauffeur-driven Mercedes swept through the school gates and glided to a halt outside the hall. Greg Armstrong emerged wearing an immaculate dark blue suit with a stripy red tie that Max had seen in countless news bulletins. The celebrity was quickly surrounded by autograph hunters,but cheerfully signed as he made his way to the top of the steps where the headmaster was waiting to greet him.

"Welcome to Bridgemont!" said Derek Aynsley as the two men shook hands.

"Picture for The Goss please, Mr. Armstrong!" shouted Ollie, aiming his camera; but before he could press the shutter, a pushy professional photographer from The Advertiser deliberately barged in front of him and ruined the shot. It was not in Sniffer Morris's nature to roll over and give up on an important story. Thrusting a hand down the back of the man's baggy jeans, he yanked on his underpants as hard as he could.

"One more, please!" he shouted over his rival's yelp of surprise. Grinning broadly, Greg repeated the handshake and Ollie had his picture.

"That young man's quite an operator!" he said as the Head whisked him off to the hall where an excited audience was eager to hear about life behind the scenes of one of Britain's best-known television news programmes.

Max sat spellbound as Greg recounted his adventures as a foreign correspondent: being shot in the leg during a fire-fight in the Middle East, escaping the clutches of a brutal dictator and witnessing the heartbreak and suffering caused by famine in Ethiopia and Sudan.

The applause was deafening when Mr. Aynsley finally led the newsreader from the hall. The time had come for Max to get his interview – and his palms were sweating as he rose from his seat clutching two biros and a small reporter's notebook.

"Good luck!" whispered Becky, giving his hand a squeeze. "And don't forget to enjoy it!"

Minutes later, he was outside the study listening to the sound of muffled conversation and trying to summon up the courage to knock. Here was the chance to meet his hero, so why was his heart beating nineteen-to-the-dozen and why did he feel like running away?

"This is ridiculous!" he told himself, giving a firm but polite rap.

"Come in, Max!" said Mr. Aynsley, ushering him inside where Greg was relaxing in a well-worn leather armchair enjoying a glass of wine.

"I'm not sure which of us should be more nervous!" laughed the newsreader, rising to shake Max's hand. "Let's plonk ourselves down on the sofa – it'll be much friendlier than talking across a desk."

The nerves quickly vanished and soon the young reporter was thoroughly enjoying himself, asking question after question and wishing the interview could go on all night.

"It'll be in The Goss tomorrow evening, Mr. Armstrong," he said as the headmaster brought their conversation to a close. "I'll e-mail you a copy if you wouldn't mind giving me the address."

"I'll look forward to that," smiled Greg. "Just send it to..." He stopped short as an idea came to him. "On second thoughts, let's forget the e-mail. It would be much nicer if you and your team could deliver my copy in person. How would you like to come to the studio on Friday and watch the Six O'Clock bulletin go out live?"

Max couldn't believe his ears.

"Would we ever!" he exclaimed, almost walking into the stationery cupboard as he fumbled for the door. "Wait till I tell the others! Thanks, Mr. Armstrong. See you on Friday!"

★★★

The rest of the week passed agonisingly slowly but, on Friday at five o'clock, the Goss team arrived at New Broadcasting House in West London where Greg's P.A.,Fiona, led them up to the Six O'Clock News control room. It was like stepping onto the bridge of the Starship Enterprise and they watched open-mouthed as the director, sitting in semi-darkness, scanned over forty television monitors as he lined up satellite reports and outside broadcasts from all over the world.

"You'd best perch at the back," whispered Fiona. "Things might get a bit hairy later on! Enjoy yourselves."

Max tapped Becky's arm and pointed to a monitor marked *Camera 3* on which they could see Greg walking onto the set and plugging in his ear-piece.

"Greg, can you hear me?" asked the director briskly.

"Loud and clear." said the presenter, closing his eyes while a make-up girl rubbed his face lightly with a small sponge.

The children sat wide-eyed with excitement as the production team bustled around them.

"Five minutes to transmission!" sounded a voice from the tannoy.

"They'll *never* be ready in time!" breathed Max as eyewitness accounts of an armed robbery were hastily pre-recorded on a link from Manchester; then the door burst open and the producer dashed in.

"Breaking news!" she announced, holding the intercom button down with her thumb. "New York has confirmed that Chuck Masters the movie star died this afternoon. He was ninety-two."

"Do we have some words for that?" asked Greg, who looked remarkably calm considering he was about to broadcast live to an audience of millions.

"They're writing them now – and there'll be an eight second film clip in the menu."

Greg nodded and made notes on his script as the minute hand moved inexorably closer to six o'clock.

"One minute to transmission!" blared the tannoy as a red light flashed urgently overhead.

Becky felt her stomach tingle as the studio went live and Greg launched calmly into the opening headlines. The next half hour seemed to race by and, all too soon, it was time for the closing sports round-up which, for the Newskids at least, began with a story very close to home.

"We start with football," announced Greg. "And as England prepares to host the World Cup, there are reports that striker Lenny Dimaggio may be signing to Gostonborough United in a record transfer deal…"

Ollie's ears pricked up. Gostonborough was their local Premiership team and he had heard rumours that the England star had been looking at expensive houses in Highmoor, a millionaires' estate less than five miles from their school. Now he knew why! If only they could get an interview with *him* for The Goss. That *would* be a scoop!

When the programme came off air, the three friends thanked Greg for a brilliant visit and headed for the station. The journey home was spent discussing every last detail of the Six O'Clock News – from the bullion raid in Manchester to the possibility of Lenny Dimaggio moving to Gostonborough United. There was even some debate as to whether Greg ever read the news wearing trainers since no-one ever saw his feet under the desk.

"Wouldn't it be awesome if we could put moving pictures into our paper!" said Ollie, breaking into a packet of Rollos. "Just *think* of the stories we could do!"

Suddenly, something exploded like a clap of thunder in Max's head and he fell silent for the rest of the journey. He could hear the others, but wasn't taking in what they said. Ollie's remark had triggered a fantastic idea – an idea that would transform the future of The Goss.

Chapter 4

SECRET MEETING

Saturday saw the last performance of 'Midnight Newsroom'. Becky looked terrific in a brand new sparkly strappy-top, but could have been wearing an old horse blanket for all the interest Max was showing as he sat in silence, waiting for the curtain to rise.

"What's up with you?" she asked. "Have Jason and Keith been on your back again?"

"It's nothing to do with them," he whispered, looking up from his programme and checking that no-one was listening. "But there *is* something – something really big that keeps rattling around in my head and won't go away..."

He was about to say more when they were interrupted by Ollie, laden with ice creams,dropping noisily into the next seat.

"What's the matter with you guys?" he said perkily. "You look as though the cat's just weed in your best trainers."

Before Becky could brain him, the house lights dimmed and the play began with Rachael making her first entrance.

"She can read my headlines *any* day of the week!" whispered Ollie, giving Max a playful dig with his elbow.

"Blokes! You're all the same!" hissed Becky who was sick and tired of Rachael Cooper, but soon had to admit that she was a *very* good actress.

Even before the final applause subsided, Max was chivvying the others to follow him home. To their surprise, instead of going in through the front door as usual, he led them urgently round the side of the house and into the garden where his father's shed loomed eerily in the moonlight under a canopy of bare, twisted branches. Max lifted the latch and the door creaked open. At the click of a switch, a single naked bulb glowed from the ceiling, casting ghostly shadows that turned people into giants and garden tools into enormous robots. He had already set out several dusty flowerpots for them to sit on and Becky was making a beeline for the cleanest one when a long cobweb brushed across her face and she let out a piercing scream.

"You'd better have a g..good reason for dragging us down here at ten thirty at night in the middle of January, Max Taylor!" she shuddered, eyeing a spider the size of a small saucer scuttling across the floor.

"I think I have," he beamed, standing excitedly in the middle of the shed. Then he made a dramatic sweeping gesture with both arms and delivered a single short announcement.

"Welcome to the studio!"

Ollie and Becky looked at each other in bewilderment.

"What *are* you on about?" asked Ollie.

"Welcome to the studio," he repeated, relieved that the moment had come to share the idea that had kept him awake most of the night. "Look, I know this might seem barmy, but it's mainly down to you, Sniff. You said something on the train yesterday that was so brilliant it almost blew me away…"

Ollie's chest swelled with pride, though he couldn't for the life of him remember what it was.

"…You said 'Wouldn't it be awesome if we could put moving pictures into The Goss.'"

There was a flicker of recollection, but it was clear that neither Ollie nor Becky was any the wiser, so Max leaned closer, his eyes darting from one to the other.

"Well…" he whispered. "Why *don't* we?"

"Why don't we *what*?" asked Becky impatiently. "You're talking rubbish, Max. How can you put moving pictures into a newsletter?"

"That's the brilliant part!" he cried. "We're going to stop producing The Goss as a newsletter and find a way of doing it on TV!"

Becky fixed him with a disbelieving stare. It was then that she noticed a familiar glint that always came into his eye when he was determined to make something happen.It was shining more brightly now than she'd ever seen it before.

"There's nothing to stop The Goss having its own website," he continued, raking his fingers through his thick blond hair. "And, if it did, we could present our stories just like they do on the Six O'Clock News. Dad's shed can be our studio and we could film our presenter with a webcam. You're always saying how much you'd like a digital *movie* camera, Sniff – well now could be the perfect time to get one. Think how cool it would be making the film reports!"

"Sick!" exclaimed Ollie, catching the wave of his enthusiasm. "And I could get one of those software packages and do my own editing."

Once he sensed the others warming to the idea, Max was unstoppable.

"We could take e-mails from punters, maybe have our own chat room," he enthused, barely pausing for breath, "And there'd be live on-the-spot reports, just like the BBC's – but instead of coming by satellite from places like Westminster and Wembley Stadium, our correspondents would be on video-phones from Goston Town Hall or the Caterpillars Football Club. What about it, Becky? You're the IT Girl. I'm relying on you to make it all work!"

"I'm n..not sure, Max," she faltered, feeling completely out of her depth and beginning to panic. "I might m..manage an 'A' in Computer Studies, but I'd need a science degree to handle something like this; and besides, The Goss doesn't officially own a P.C. yet!"

Before he could reply, she sprang to her feet, her eyes wide and scared.

"Shhhh!" she hissed. "There's someone outside!"

"It's nothing to worry about, Becky..." assured Max, but she silenced him with a cautionary finger. Suddenly, there was a loud clang and a torch beam flared through the window. Her heart was pounding now and Ollie grabbed a rake as the latch clicked upwards and the door began to open.

"Have we come to the right place?" asked a familiar voice.

Ollie and Becky stared in amazement as into the light stepped Rachael Cooper, still wearing full stage make-up, followed by Akbar Khan, better known as 'Sparks', techno-wizard of the school drama club.

"Sorry to have kept all this so quiet," apologised Max. "I tried to tell you before the play started, Becky, but didn't want anyone to overhear. Oh – you haven't met Rachael and Akbar properly, have you…?"

"Hi…" she said limply, staring at Rachael's false eye lashes and wondering what her own mother would say if *she* were to go out looking like that; then, taking a grip on herself, she remembered to add: "Congratulations on the play. You were awesome."

"That's sweet of you," replied Rachael flashing her a dazzling smile. "And congratulations on the Environment Awareness website. You're just as brilliant as Max said you were."

Becky found the compliment disarming. Perhaps Rachael wasn't the self-centred 'luvvie' she'd imagined; but what was she doing in Max's garden shed in the middle of the night when she should have been the toast of the after-show party? Sparks quickly gave a clue.

"When you asked if I could help build a television studio, I wasn't expecting it to be in a garden shed, Max," he said, searching around for power points.

Suddenly, everything began to make sense and Becky felt hurt that Max had kept the idea a secret from his closest friends, but chosen to share it with two people he hardly knew.

"I wonder if anyone has given any thought to who the *presenter* on this TV station might be?" she asked with heavy sarcasm, addressing Ollie, but aiming the question squarely at Max.

Rachael knew exactly what Becky meant and was quick to reassure her.

"Oh, I know as much as you do," she explained. "All Max said was that there may be an opportunity for an anchor-person in a new community TV station; but he told me that nothing could happen unless you and Ollie were happy with the choice. I guess tonight was my audition. I hope I passed."

Becky felt slightly less hostile although, after years of being the only girl in the team, the prospect of Rachael muscling in made her feel insecure and quite jealous; but as Max had so clearly set his heart on this idea, she decided to set her own feelings aside and help make it work.

"You passed alright, Rachael," she said, putting on a brave smile. "Welcome to the team."

Rachael squealed with delight, hugging Becky and kissing the air on both sides of her face.

"We're lucky to have those wooden beams across the ceiling," interrupted Sparks,climbing down from Mr. Taylor's step-ladder and wiping dust from his hands. "I can use the one over the geranium pots to hang a backcloth for the news desk and the one above the door to fix studio lights. Power's going to be a problem – there's only one socket and we'll need at least two once the sound and lighting desks are working – and then there's the P.C. to run…"

Ollie and Becky stared at each other. Where was all

this equipment going to come from? Even Max swallowed hard. He was hoping to cover the cost with a few weeks' allowance, but it now looked as though he'd need to take out a bank loan.

"I don't want to throw spanners in the works," said Ollie. "But don't you think we might be biting off a bit more than we can chew? Even if we can get all this stuff, supposing your dad won't *lend* us his shed?"

Max was only too aware that if his father said no, the whole plan was dead in the water. Becky knew it too. She also knew that Mr. Taylor had a soft spot for her and that the chances of persuading him might be better if she and Max presented a united front.

"Why don't we ask him now, Max," she said. "At least we'll know where we stand."

Max squeezed her arm as they made their way back up the garden towards the house.

"I know I can be a prat when I get carried away with things," he said. "What would I do without you, Becky? You're a star!"

Becky glowed. She loved Max paying her compliments, but wished he'd do it more often when he *didn't* need her help.

The two friends entered the kitchen and walked into the hall where a light was shining under Mr. Taylor's study door. They could hear the faint clacking of a computer keyboard punctuated by an occasional cry of frustration.

"Oh no!" groaned Max. "He's having a bad P.C. day!"

"Come on!" urged Becky. "He won't eat us. Last one in's a sissy!" Then they traded high fives and opened the door.

"Hi, dad!" said Max cheerfully. "What's going on?"

"Bring back pen and ink!" grumbled Mr. Taylor. "Whatever you want will have to wait till tomorrow, Max. I'm trying to finish some illustrated scripts and the computer's strangling any creativity I've got left. All of us at the agency were given fancy new laptops today – and I haven't got the hang of this beast yet!"

"Mr. Taylor..." purred Becky, seizing her opportunity. "If I *promise* to set up your laptop and g..give you as *many* computer lessons as you like, is there any chance that you'd consider..." She paused, trying not to stumble over her words. "...d..donating your old P.C. to The Goss?"

"I've a good mind to donate it to the local rubbish tip at the moment," said Mr. Taylor, only half listening as he tried to get rid of an animated paint brush that kept winking at him as it swished tauntingly across the screen.

"We have this major plan, you see," she persisted, deftly removing it and determined to keep his attention. "We want to run The Goss as a TV station on the internet. It was Max's idea and I think you should be very proud of him for thinking it up."

Suddenly, Mr. Taylor stopped what he was doing. They had his undivided attention now, but he was well and truly on his guard.

"And where does my computer fit into this?" he asked suspiciously.

"We'll n..need it in our studio."

"Studio?" he repeated, completely forgetting the half-finished scripts. "Even if I agree to 'donate' my old P.C., where on earth are you three going to get a television studio?"

There was a pause, then Max took over.

"Well," he began, trying to stay cool and play down the favour he was about to ask."We thought your garden shed might be quite good..."

"Oh, did you now?" said Mr. Taylor leaning back in utter astonishment. "Perhaps you'd like me to sell the house and put the money down as a deposit on the James Bond Stage at Pinewood?"

The children sensed disaster.

"I know it's a big ask, dad," pleaded Max. "But I really believe in this. It would help us connect with the community in a way we've never done before. But if it's going to cause grief, then we'll just have to find somewhere else or give the whole thing up."

At that moment, Nick Taylor caught the hope and conviction in his son's eyes and knew immediately that this was no hare-brained stunt. It mattered deeply to Max and the least he could do was to take it seriously. He thought hard for a moment or two, then drained his coffee mug.

"Well," he said quietly, "I may be computer-illiterate, but I'm also an advertising man who knows a good idea when he hears one." Max exchanged glances with Becky as his father rose and paced the room, hands buried deep in his trouser pockets. "I'll need to talk to mum about this, but I think you may be on to something and I'll go along with it on four conditions. First of all, this television station mustn't get in the way of your school work. If that happens, we'll close the whole thing down straight away, is that clearly understood?"

Max nodded.

"Secondly, it will be your responsibility to find a safe, dry home for all the garden tools and furniture."

A harder nod.

"Thirdly, as payment in kind, I would like you and your team to cut the grass and keep the flowerbeds weeded all year round..."

A slightly less enthusiastic nod – then Mr. Taylor stopped dead in his tracks.

"What's the fourth condition, Mr. T.?" asked Becky, hanging on his every word.

"Ah, yes, the fourth," he murmured, rubbing his chin and looking very serious indeed.Then he grinned broadly. "When do I get my first computer lesson?"

Chapter 5

MAKING IT HAPPEN

Becky couldn't sleep. Her mind was a tangle of problems and, as she grappled with one, others grew – just like Hercules cutting off the Hydra's monstrous heads. Why had no-one listened when she said she felt out of her depth?

Suddenly, the landing light came on and her mother came quietly into the room.

"What's the matter, love?" she whispered, perching on the edge of the bed. "It's three o'clock in the morning."

"It's The Goss," sniffed Becky. "Max wants to turn it into a TV station on the web and they're relying on me to d..design the site. But I don't think I can do it, mum – and it will be all my fault if everything goes wrong. They'll think I'm useless and Max will never speak to me again…" Then she burst into tears and flung herself into her mother's arms.

Mrs. Roberts gently stroked her hair, imparting the safe, reassuring feeling Becky remembered as a little girl when she was teased about her stammer in primary school.

"Who says it's all going to go wrong?" she said. "And there's no reason why you should take all the responsibility if it does. The Goss is a team effort and if you have worries, you must share them with Max. He's sure to understand. Now try and get some sleep. I promise things will seem much brighter in the morning."

She clung to her mother for a moment or two, then slipped back under the duvet. By the time her head touched the pillow, she was fast asleep.

★★★

At eight o'clock next morning, Becky arrived at the Taylors' house prepared to share all her misgivings with Max. She felt much happier as she rang the bell, but her face fell when Rachael Cooper answered the door.

"Hi, Becky!" she gushed. "I just stopped by to give Max a hand in the shed. I'm glad you're here because he's feeling kind of low and I'm running out of ways of cheering him up."

Becky felt a surge of resentment. The Taylor household had always been her second home, but now she felt like an outsider. What right had Rachael to be cheering Max up when she had only just joined the team? What was she doing at his house so early? Why was she there at all?

Rachael led the way into the back garden where Max was busy clearing out the shed.

"How does it feel being a TV executive?" joked Becky, trying to hide her feelings.

"It makes me feel like being a milkman instead," he said gloomily. "I'm not so sure that this idea is going to work, Becky."

"Why not?" she asked in surprise. "You were so pumped up about it last night."

"Oh, I'm still pumped up," he sighed. "But I'm also broke. Sparks says it'll cost a fortune just to rewire the shed – and that's before we think about webcams, videophones, movie cameras...do you want the whole list?"

This news could have scotched all her worries, but instead of relief, Becky felt only disappointment. The truth was that she believed in Max's idea just as strongly as he believed in it himself and was about to say so when Rachael butted in.

"What we need are sponsors!" she declared. "Why don't you appeal to your readers? There are over two hundred families in this street. The Goss gives them all the local news they could want, advertises their events – and doesn't cost them a cent. There must be some generous electricians and computer buffs around here who'd be happy to offer us their services for free. It's called 'putting something back into the community'."

Max began to take heart.

"Rachael, I could kiss you!" he exclaimed. "It's so obvious, it's completely brilliant!"

Rachael wasn't sure whether to take this as a compliment or an insult, while Becky was horrified that her closest friend was even *thinking* of kissing the new girl on the block.

"Let's go!" he shouted, like a sergeant major drilling a bunch of new recruits. "Time to get this show on the road!"

Soon, the little army was on the march, carrying the contents of Mr. Taylor's shed to a neighbour's empty garage for safe-keeping. Max was wheeling the barbecue piled high with bags of charcoal while Becky carried an armful of garden tools and Rachael brought up the rear with a stack of plastic chairs. Suddenly, a voice boomed across the garden and they clattered into each other as Ollie appeared behind a rhododendron bush.

"Smile!" he yelled. "You've all been framed!"

"Leave it out, Sniff!" called Max. "Why don't you give us a hand instead of taking photographs?"

"Who says I'm taking photographs?" he teased, grinning broadly as he raised his right hand. Max gasped at what he saw. Instead of his trusty stills camera, Ollie was clutching a brand new camcorder.

"Where did that come from?" asked Becky in amazement.

"My dad had it in the shop as a demonstration model," said Ollie proudly. "But the manufacturers have come up with a new design so he's given it to me on permanent loan! I've been trying it out on Mrs. Foster's baby – and I just got some great shots of you guys traipsing up the garden like an advert for B & Q!"

Ollie's news gave Max such a boost that he became quite manic.

"I'm going to write an appeal for sponsors right now!" he said, abandoning the barbecue and heading towards the house. "We'll put it in this Wednesday's edition. With luck, we'll have the TV station up and running inside a month!"

Warning bells were sounding in Becky's head. She

knew how impulsive he could be when he was in one of his hyper-moods.

"Isn't that a b..bit hasty?" she called. "Think what idiots we'll look if it all goes pear-shaped..."

But she was too late. He was already poring over the kitchen calendar.

"This is a hot project!" he shouted, grabbing a pencil from the sideboard and dashing back outside. "But no-one will respond if they don't sense the urgency." Then he began to scribble on a half-empty charcoal bag adding: "And I've just thought of a great headline: '*NEWSKIDS ON THE NET! The Goss needs YOUR help to launch the street's own TV news service. Going live on February 26th.*' Move over, Greg Armstrong! We're on our way!"

***

Becky took the long way home. Everything was happening too fast and she needed time to think. By the time she reached the end of Sheraton Street, she had made up her mind to tell Max that the TV project was too much for her and that it would be fairer on the whole team if they brought in someone more experienced. Turning unhappily into Tittlemarsh Avenue, she spotted a familiar black bicycle propped up in a porch. The cycle clips and goggles hanging from the handlebars confirmed her suspicion: it was the home of Charles Dudgeon. Somehow, she felt drawn towards the green front door and, before she knew it, had given the bell a firm shove, bringing Bridgemont's Head of I.C.T. thundering downstairs wearing green Wellington boots, cricket flannels and a rather wet Aston Villa football shirt.

"Bless my soul! Becky Roberts!" he exclaimed, drying his hands on an old pair of pyjama bottoms. "You've caught me changing a washer in the bathroom. Come in. What can I do for you?"

Ensconced in a corner of his sitting room, Becky poured out her concerns while Mr.Dudgeon listened with mounting interest, making notes on the back of an envelope.

"This isn't going to be easy," he murmured. "But it's certainly possible."

She saw a tiny glimmer of hope.

"The best way would be to create a website, just like the one we made at school.During the week, it would carry all your local stories, photos and captions. They could be updated every day if you wished. Then, on Wednesdays, you'll need a link to the live webcast."

He paused, fixing her with a schoolmasterly stare until he was sure that she had followed what he'd said.

"That's the good news," he continued, shifting awkwardly in his squeaky chair. "The bad news is that if this TV station is to stream a webcam and film reports, carry live video calls *and* handle e-mails and a chat room, you're going to need at least one extra P.C."

Becky's fragile hopes were suddenly dashed. It was sheer luck that they had *one* P.C. The chances of getting a second were as likely as winning the National Lottery without a ticket. Mr. Dudgeon could see that she was about to cry and began to rub his chin as if, by doing so, he would hold back the tears.

"Don't be upset," he said. "It's always darkest before

the dawn. I think this is a terrific idea and I'm sure that Mr. Aynsley would want me to support it in any way I can. You're welcome to borrow a P.C. from school – and I'll even throw in my webcam if it would help."

Becky wanted to scream with delight and it was all she could do not to hug him as he escorted her back into the hallway.

"There's one other thing you might consider," he suggested, struggling to open the front door which finally yielded to a sharp kick from the toe of his boot. "Your project would make a terrific story for Cyber-Mania Magazine. Thousands of young people read it. You never know, one of them may have a high definition mobile video-phone going cheap!"

"Wicked idea, Mr. Dudgeon!" said Becky, not quite knowing how to thank him. "You're a legend! See you in class tomorrow!"

She was starting to enjoy her role in this project – and felt determined to play it well!

★★★

At 7.03 on Wednesday, January 29th, Max hit 'send' on edition 25 of The Goss. The headline '*NEWSKIDS ON THE NET – GOING LIVE ON FEBRUARY 26TH*' was a scary leap into the unknown for every member of the team and their future in television now lay entirely in their readers' hands. Becky knew they were in for a white-knuckle ride over the next few weeks and decided to keep a diary:

FRIDAY, JANUARY 31ST

Ring Cyber-Mania Magazine. They want to send writer and photographer when we're fitting out studio and installing P.Cs. We have to do this on Saturday, February 15th to meet their deadline. That's two weeks away. Eeek!Mr. Partridge the electrician phones. He'll rewire studio for free because he once sold his motor scooter through The Goss and thinks we do a great job. Top news! Rude text arrives. Probably from Keith Pratt and Jason Steed. Ignore it

SATURDAY, FEBRUARY 1ST

Elderly man rings looking for rod suitable for catching carp. Thought Newskidson the Net was a fishing magazine. Say sorry can't help.Ollie scrounges roll of pale blue backing paper from Say Cheese portrait studio. It's big enough to be the background for our set. Sparks persuades school drama club to lend sound and lighting consoles. So far, so good! Design home page using Sniff's photographs as links to stories. Max thinks it's great and calls me a genius. Nice to be appreciated but still don't know how to cope with the million-and-one other things the site is meant to do...another sleepless night.

SUNDAY, FEBRUARY 2ND

Paint shed. Rachael worried about getting emulsion on designer jeans. Why is she wearing them to paint a shed, that's what I'd like to know? All looks great but will take a week to get rid of smell. Bed 11.30 p.m. – knackered!

WEDNESDAY, FEBRUARY 5TH

Cyber-Mania ring. An internet service provider has offered us free web space and our own address: newskidsonthenet.co.uk It's all happening!!

THURSDAY, FEBRUARY 6TH

Just when everything going well, realise haven't got a news desk and Cyber-Mania is coming on Saturday week. Decide to put S.O.S. in next Wednesday's Goss.

MONDAY, FEBRUARY 10TH

Keep falling asleep and forgetting to write up diary. Will do better tomorrow.

TUESDAY, FEBRUARY 11TH

2 weeks and 1 day to first show (Scareeeee!). Discuss live studio events and decide to have a Superpets competition. Will hold auditions on Saturday while Max's parents are away. School P.C. hasn't arrived. No webcam. No high definition video-mobile. Everything else hunky dory…!

WEDNESDAY, FEBRUARY 12TH

Life really hectic producing this week's Goss and setting up Newskids at same time. Parents think we're barmy. Advertise for news desk and talented pets.

THURSDAY, FEBRUARY 13TH

Panic phone call from Rachael who has nothing to wear for the Cyber-Mania photo shoot. Think of suggesting paper bag over head, but chicken out and promise to take her shopping.

FRIDAY, FEBRUARY 14TH

Go shopping with Rachael after school. Groovy Chicks offer to lend her some outfits if we mention them on programme. Rachael wants a very short skirt for Saturday. I say no-one will see her legs under the desk, but she insists…still, I expect the boys will like it. Ollie and Sparks collect two desks. Big one gets stuck in doorway trapping Ollie in shed. Have to take door off to release him. Desk looks naff anyway, but smaller one O.K. Another rude text arrives.

SATURDAY, FEBRUARY 15TH

Big day. Cyber-Mania team turns up just as Superpets arrive to audition. Footballing Irish Wolf Hound goes berserk and Charlie Warren's break-dancing Jack Russell bites photographer who has to have Tetanus jab. Sparks rigs backdrop and studio lamps. Rachael thinks lighting too harsh. Suggest it will hide her wrinkles. She tells me not to be silly, but rushes off to find a mirror…Mr. Dudgeon arrives to help install P.Cs. Drills through a power cable. His hair stands on end and all lights fuse. Chaos. Cyber-Mania get great photos.

SUNDAY, FEBRUARY 16TH

Local electronics chain store donates state-of-the-art webcam complete with tripod and zoom lens. Rachael thinks it makes her look fat. Phones and sound desk don't work and Ollie has no editing kit. Why did we start this…?

MONDAY, FEBRUARY 17TH

Select finalists for Superpets competition: Sandy Huxtable (13) with Hamish, his singing West Highland terrier, Tracey Metcalfe (7) with Chubby the skateboarding hamster (sweet!) and Tom Clutterbuck who puts ferrets down his trousers. (Yuk!)

WEDNESDAY, FEBRUARY 19TH

Last ever edition of The Goss. Feel sad and excited at the same time. Banner headline: Coming Next Wednesday – Newskids on the Net. Live web-cast 7 – 8 p.m. Everyone feeling the pressure now. Local paper rings. They want to run article on us the day we go on line. Ollie's chocolate consumption reaches new heights! Cyber-Mania article out today. We're on the front cover and there's a centre-page photo-spread. Mobile company offers quality video-phone. Max says it's only to be used for the station – not gossiping with mates. He can be sooooooo bossy sometimes!

FRIDAY, FEBRUARY 21ST

Ollie shoots first video report of Glitz 'n' Grunge fashion show at the Civic Hall. Smoke machine goes off unexpectedly while winning outfit is on the catwalk. Audience thinks hall is on fire and evacuates…very funny!

Sunday, February 23rd

Not much to laugh at now. We're live in three days time. P.Cs still not working and there aren't enough stories to fill a whole hour. Help…!

Chapter 6

GOING LIVE!

'*NEWSKIDS GO LIVE – TONIGHT!*' proclaimed the headline in The Gazette on Wednesday, February 26th. There was no more room for mistakes. In less than an hour, most of Goston would be glued to its P.Cs expecting a show that lived up to all the hype and publicity.

The transformation of the garden shed was incredible. From beams where watering cans and hedge clippers once hung, studio lamps were blazing down on an elegant, pale blue set where *NEWSKIDS ON THE NET*, painted in gold by a local sign-writer, glinted across the front of the news desk. Suddenly, everything had become very real, very grown-up and very scary.

"How much longer are you going to be on the school P.C.?" called Sparks as Ollie struggled to edit the vicar's appeal for new members of the church choir. "It's quarter past six. If Becky and I can't get to the equipment soon, we'll never be on line at seven!"

Ollie didn't need reminding that time was running out, but the faster he tried to work,the more mistakes he was making – and the pressure was beginning to tell.

"I don't know why we're bothering with the vicar's choir anyway," he snapped. "Nobody will want to join. They're nothing but a crowd of boring old busybodies who can't sing…"

He stopped short as, by a disastrous piece of timing, the Reverend Peters sidled into the shed, pretending not to have heard.

"Well, well, Oliver Morris," he said. "I trust I haven't chosen a bad moment to drop in?"

"Not at all, Reverend Peters," interrupted Max, springing to the rescue. "This is a big day for us and things are a bit tense, I'm afraid."

"Quite understandable, Max," said the elderly clergyman, raising a hand in a gesture of forgiveness. "I only stopped by to wish you the best of luck and to say thanks for making the appeal. I'm relying on it to beef up the baritone section at St. Benedict's!"

The sound desk chose that moment to emit an ear-splitting shriek that gave the vicar such a shock that he leapt outside and beat a hasty retreat up the garden.

With forty minutes to go, Becky was busily checking the guest list and labelling chairs for everyone to sit on.

"Thanks for everything," said Max, giving her a hug. "And however well or badly the show goes tonight, I want you to know that we'd never have got this far without you."

Before she could respond, Rachael made her entrance, using the latest edition of Teen Vogue to shield her new haircut from the gusting wind. She was wearing a stunning cream trouser suit that framed a pale pink tee shirt under its well-cut jacket.

"How do I look?" she said, twirling like a model as she took her place at the news desk.

"Fantastic!" said Max, drawing up two more chairs so that he and Becky could brief her on the evening's stories. "We'll open with your interview with Councillor Lewis. He's leading a march down Goston High Street on Saturday morning. They're protesting about the new motorway extension."

"What background do we have?" she asked, sounding confident and professional.

"Lewis thinks it's being built too close to the p..park," explained Becky, glancing at her notes. "The contractors are moving in on Monday and he's threatening to chain himself to a bulldozer to stop them starting work. He'll go to jail if necessary. There could be up to five hundred demonstrators and their slogan is *'NO-WAY MOTO-WAY'."*

"I hope he'll be here in good time," frowned Max, checking the schedule. "It's our main story."

"I've just checked with his secretary," Becky assured him. "She promised me six thirty latest. Don't worry, Max. He'll be here."

"How long do you want the interview to run?" asked Rachael, managing to take everything in and apply lipstick and blusher at the same time.

"Ten minutes tops," Max replied. "We'll follow it with Ollie's fashion film, then you can introduce Hamish the West Highland terrier who sings the theme from 'Emmerdale'."

Rachael looked worried.

"And what am I supposed to do if he *doesn't* sing the theme from 'Emmerdale'?" she asked. "You know what they say about working with animals and children."

"We've already thought that through," said Becky, not wanting to be caught out. "If Hamish misbehaves, we'll g..go straight to the pre-recorded church choir appeal."

"Then it's Tom Clutterbuck," continued Max, keeping an eye on the time. "He's the man who puts ferrets down his trousers."

Rachael shot him a horrified glance, almost poking the mascara brush into her eye as Mr. Taylor came breathlessly into the studio clutching a copy of The Goston Evening News.

"Sorry to butt in," he panted. "I thought you should see this. I've run all the way from the station."

Max's heart raced as he read the front page headline: '*DIMAGGIO ON THE MOVE!*'

"It looks as though Greg Armstrong's prediction was right," he exclaimed, skimming the story. "Lenny's free to join Goston United, but he and his manager are still arguing over terms. They're meeting the board tonight at seven. How long would it take you to cycle to the ground, Sniff? We're live in fifteen minutes."

"If there's a chance of interviewing Lenny Dimaggio, I'll be there in ten!" he replied.

"Don't go breaking your neck," warned Max. "And take the video-phone with you. We'll take a live report."

"Safe!" said Ollie, zipping up his anorak and

turning to Sparks. "My film reports are all ready to go. Insert one is the fashion story, number two is the vicar's appeal and three is my practice tape." Then he grabbed the video-phone and made for the door, braying "Good luck, darlings!" in an over-the-top theatrical voice before setting off on his first ever outside broadcast.

With five minutes to go, there was a clap of thunder and Goston was battered by a torrential storm. Their first guest still hadn't arrived and Max was becoming more and more agitated when suddenly the studio door almost flew off its hinges. He looked up, expecting to see Councillor Lewis, but instead his mother appeared clutching a plastic umbrella blown inside out by the wind.

"A Mr. Clutterbuck has arrived with a box full of ferrets," she said, wrinkling her nose in disgust. "I don't want them in the house, so I've brought him straight down here."

A tall, red-faced Yorkshireman stooped under the door frame and shook water from his cap all over Rachael's suit.

"Evenin' all," he said cheerily, setting down a large wooden crate. "I need to get 'em acclimatised. Ferrets can be very temperamental in front o' strangers, you know."

While Rachael gave her wet jacket a frantic blast with the hair dryer, Sparks led Tom Clutterbuck to a stool in the corner where he prepared for his performance by tying string round the knees of his loose-fitting corduroy trousers.

"What's happened to Lewis?" called Max, checking

his watch for the umpteenth time. "We're live in three minutes."

"I'm t..talking to his P.A. now," replied Becky who had the phone clamped to her ear. Then her jaw dropped. "He's stuck in traffic..."

"You're having a laugh!" he groaned, trying hard not to let his own anxiety get to the rest of the team.

By one minute to seven, the atmosphere had reached fever pitch. Guests were packed in like sardines and the smell of wet, panting animals hung in the air. Last to arrive was Chubby the skateboarding hamster whose owner, little Tracey Metcalfe, had brought her two brothers to cheer him on in the Superpets competition; but there was still no sign of Councillor Lewis.

"Thirty seconds to webcast!" warned Becky. "Quiet in the studio!"

"We'll have to start without him!" cried Max. "Stand by with the fashion film, Sparks. Good luck, Rachael! You're going to be great!"

Rachael fluffed up her hair as Sparks framed her in the viewfinder and focused the webcam.

"Ten seconds!" called Becky, catching Max's eye. The taut smile told her that he was far from confident, but there was no turning back and the next hour would determine whether they became local heroes or village idiots.

The news jingle sounded and Rachael Cooper smiled at the camera, looking calm and relaxed as Newskids on the Net went live for the first time.

"Good evening, and welcome to the programme," she said. "Today, Goston's first community television service went on line – and you're watching it. The main stories tonight: 'No-Way Moto-way' – we talk to the councillor who's prepared to go to jail to keep the M64 away from Goston Park; 'Stars With Fur In Their Eyes' – our search for the town's Superpet; and will England striker, Lenny Dimaggio, sign for Gostonborough United in this World Cup year? But first – fashion..."

Ollie was soaked to the skin by the time he reached Gostonborough United's stadium. Parking his bike, he stared apprehensively at the hordes of unsmiling journalists and film crews huddling under golfing umbrellas as they talked to their news desks on mobile phones. He knew that the others were relying on him for the Dimaggio story, but wondered what chance a fourteen-year-old stood of getting an interview with a soccer legend against the army of hardened professionals massing in the car park. Suddenly, the video-phone rang. It was Max.

"We've got trouble, Sniff!" he said. "Lewis hasn't turned up and there are only two minutes left on the fashion piece. I'm worried we're going to run out of stories. What can you give us on Dimaggio?"

"The word is that he'll be here in about ten minutes," shouted Ollie, trying to make himself heard above the storm. "Nobody knows whether he'll stop and talk, but I'll get what I can."

Max checked that Sparks was happy with the signal, then turned to Rachael.

"Introduce the singing terrier next," he directed. "We'll follow it with the vicar's choir appeal and then you can go live to Sniff at the ground."

The car park was ablaze with TV lights as the professionals braced themselves for the inevitable push and shove when the striker arrived. Ollie was clinging to the hope that a football hero wouldn't turn down a young autograph hunter in front of the national press and decided to approach Dimaggio not as a journalist, but as a young fan. Perhaps the star would answer a question or two while he signed.

Back in the studio, things were going from bad to worse. Hamish the singing Westie had lost his voice and no amount of coaxing would get the contrary creature to perform.Max gazed longingly at the door, praying for Councillor Lewis to walk through it. He didn't.

"Perhaps Hamish is saving himself for later in the show," Rachael ad libbed, moving quickly on to the next story. "But right now, here's Reverend Peters with an appeal on behalf of the St. Benedict's church choir."

Sparks selected 'insert two' and clicked 'play'; but instead of the vicar, a plump baby boy appeared on the screen, as naked as the day he was born and sitting on a potty.

"Oh, no!" wailed Max, clutching his head as the tot made a succession of revolting noises."That's Mrs. Foster's son! This must be Sniff's practice tape. What's going on?"

"It's not my fault!" protested Sparks. "Ollie must have got his insert numbers mixed up."

"What do I do next?" hissed Rachael off camera, looking a good deal less composed."I can't talk to myself for the next half hour!"

Max sensed the programme falling apart and called across to Becky.

"Try to get Ollie on video-phone! Tell him this is an emergency and we need something straight away."

While Becky called the number, Rachael took a sip of water and faced the camera,making a huge effort to look calm and relaxed as the baby gave a defiant wiggle and faded from the screen.

"We'll get to the bottom of that tiny problem as soon as possible," she said with a self-conscious giggle. "Meanwhile, England star Lenny Dimaggio and his manager are expected at any moment for a meeting with Gostonborough United's board. So let's cross live to our own Premiership ground and get the latest from Newskids' sports reporter, Ollie Morris."

Holding the video-phone at arms length, Ollie talked into the camera, trying to keep the lashing rain out of the lens.

"Thanks, Rachael," he said. "Tonight's meeting could be as stormy as the weather.The question is what sort of money will secure the super-striker for Gostonborough in this World Cup year…?"

At that moment, his voice was drowned out by a green Aston Martin roaring into the car park. Screeching to a halt, Dimaggio flung open the driver's door and showed no remorse as a photographer was knocked to the ground. Ollie held the mobile as high as he could as the striker and his manager emerged, trying to keep pace with them as they pushed aggressively through the crowd.

"This is amazing stuff!" cried Max, watching the star's shaven head bobbing through a forest of cameras and microphones while portable TV lights glinted on the trademark cluster of rings that studded his left ear. There was uproar as reporters shouted questions from all sides; but Ollie was pushed further and further towards the back of the scrum until his only option was to run ahead and film the seething mob moving towards the stadium. He had just made his move when the striker and his manager broke free and headed straight towards him. Seizing his chance, he dashed forward and offered the autograph book and pen.

"What sort of a deal are you after, Lenny?" he shouted, pointing the video-phone at the star's wet, angry face; but Dimaggio curled his lip and pushed him aside.

He tried again.

"Ollie Morris from Newskids on the Net..."

This time the player's manager intervened, wrenching the mobile from his hand and hurling it to the ground.

"Call him back!" shouted Max as the signal died. "Make sure he's O.K. Stand by the performing ferrets!"

Tom Clutterbuck unfastened the cage and was awaiting his cue to introduce the razor-toothed creatures into his trousers when, thankfully, Councillor Lewis arrived.

"No-way Moto-way," announced Rachael, going straight into the introduction as Becky wheeled him into the hot seat. "That's the slogan for Saturday's demonstration against the new M64 extension..."

Max slumped back in his chair and wiped the perspiration from his forehead.Everyone was shattered after the programme's hair-raising start and, as the councillor got into his stride, they began to collect their thoughts – but the relief was short-lived.The interview had been running less than three minutes when there was a rapid movement under Sparks' chair. Max thought his eyes were playing him tricks, but whenTom Clutterbuck started to crawl across the floor, he knew that something was amiss.

"Oh, no!" he groaned."The ferrets are loose!"

Little Tracey Metcalfe tightened her grip on Chubby the skateboarding hamster as the three wiry creatures darted from under the control desk, twitching their whiskers and showing rows of needle-sharp teeth.

"Councillor Lewis," continued Rachael, completely unaware of the drama unfolding down below. "It has been reported that you would chain yourself to a mechanical digger to prevent this motorway going through. Is that true?"

Instead of answering her question, Mr. Lewis let out a high-pitched shriek and leapt onto the news desk, kicking his legs in the air like a demented tap dancer until one of the ferrets dropped from his trouser leg and landed in Rachael's lap. Rachael Cooper had proved that she could cope with most of the problems live television could throw at her, but ferrets were beyond the pale. She fled screaming from the studio as Hamish the singing Westie slipped his lead and chased the long, wriggling creatures round the shed, barking for all he was worth. Max made a dive for the dog's collar but, missing his footing, sailed over the news desk, bringing a spotlight and most of the scenery crashing to the floor. Sparks zoomed the camera in on his face as it peered dazedly over the desk top, glasses wildly askew.

"That's the end of the first edition of Newkids on the Net," he spluttered, knowing that the programme had been a disaster from beginning to end and wondering what had possessed him to think that a group of kids could run a television station in the first place. "I hope you'll join us at the same time next week...but we won't blame you if you don't... er... Goodnight."

Two of the ferrets scampered in front of his nose with Hamish in hot pursuit. They flew out into the garden, demolishing the webcam as they went – then the screen went blank.

Chapter 7

MISSING

It was Max's turn for a troubled night. The evening's disaster gnawed at his mind, tormenting him with one nightmare after another: Reverend Peters loomed out of the darkness conducting a choir of West Highland terriers; Councillor Lewis led a protest march of ferrets along the M64 and, laughing demonically, Keith Pratt and Jason Steed crashed Lenny Dimaggio's Aston Martin into the studio at ninety miles-an-hour. The impact jerked him awake and he sprang bolt upright, his hair and pyjamas soaked with sweat.

He glanced at the radio alarm. It was 6 a.m. In two hours they would have to face the taunts and sniggers on the school bus. Dressing quickly, he crept downstairs and went out into the garden. The frozen grass crunched underfoot as he made his way to the shed, feeling like a criminal returning to the scene of some grizzly crime. Slowly, he picked up the overturned chairs and pulled the crumpled paper backcloth away from the news desk, tearing off a small corner to compose a letter to the neighbours.

Dear former viewers,

There are no excuses for the pathetic apology for a television programme we put out last night. I promise it will never happen again…

The door catch rattled and he looked up, screwing the note into a ball as Becky came in.

"I thought I might find you here," she said, clambering over a fallen lighting stand."I couldn't sleep either."

"I'm surprised you're still speaking to me," said a shamefaced Max. "I should be locked up for forcing you guys into this."

"Don't be an idiot!" she smiled, trying to hide her own disappointment. "There isn't a single one of us who didn't get a buzz out of putting Newskids on the Net together – even if it did turn out to be the disaster of the year."

For a moment or two, they stood in silence, remembering the fun and excitement of the last few weeks; then Ollie appeared, clutching what was left of the video-phone.

"Anyone got any Superglue?" he asked. "Lenny Dimaggio's manager was a bit heavy-handed putting the phone down!"

Max felt better knowing that his two best friends were still there for him – and at least the phone was insured; so while he and Ollie assessed the damage, Becky booted up one of the P.Cs. She was expecting some messages of complaint, but almost fainted when she saw what was waiting for them in the inbox.

"I d..don't believe this!" she gasped. "There are twelve hundred e-mails in here!"

"It can't have been *that* bad!" cried Ollie, leaping over to her with a horrified Max hard on his heels.

"This one's from Newcastle!" she said, shaking with excitement as she read aloud:"Brilliant! Your show was *much* better than the telly. Please, please do it again next Wednesday. I shall tell all my friends to watch. Love from Sharon."

"And this one's from Southend," cried Ollie in delight. "They should keep a cage-full of ferrets in the House of Commons so that M.Ps can have them put down their trousers whenever they tell porkies. Keep up the good work from Trevor."

"Newskids is the coolest site around," quoted Max, not knowing whether to laugh or cry. "Better than any reality show. Can't wait to see what happens in Goston next week. L O L. Fidelma from Belfast.

"Can our basset-hound Horatio sing on your show?" giggled Becky, taking her turn."He always joins in when my dad plays his opera C.Ds. C U on line next Wednesday! Tommo, the Liverpool Legend."

The only complaint was from Melissa Thompson from the local primary school who was disappointed that the skateboarding hamster had been dropped from the programme and wanted it invited back next week.

The three friends stared at each other in amazement. The Cyber-Mania article had delivered more than free web space and a high definition video-phone – it had brought them a nationwide audience that had clearly liked what it had seen.

"Don't ask me how," said Max, "but we've got a hit on our hands! A big, fat,mega-stonking hit!"

Suddenly, they were laughing and screaming like

four-year-olds, dancing round the studio and singing "Congratulations" at the tops of their voices until Max's dad appeared wearing an overcoat over his pyjamas.

"Don't tell me you're hosting the Eurovision Song Contest next!" he smiled. "I just popped down to say that three members of Goston Operatic Society have phoned. They want to join the vicar's choir. This TV station of yours seems to have hit the spot – but isn't it about time you three were off to school?"

Max looked at his watch. The bus was due in five minutes.

"Dad's right, guys!" he said. "Time to face the music!"

As they hurried to the bus stop, a lone figure, head bowed and overcoat collar covering its mouth and chin, shuffled out of Henley Gardens and hovered a few yards behind them.

"Do you guys mind if I tag along?" whispered a girl's voice. "I don't think I could handle the humiliation by myself." It was Rachael. Her eyes were hidden behind an enormous pair of sunglasses and she wore a thick, woolly hat pulled down over her ears.

"Who says we're going to be humiliated?" asked Max as three juniors, who had seen straight through the disguise, raced up to her, tearing pages from their exercise books.

"Great show!" said one, handing over a silver glitter pen. "Can I have your autograph?"

Rachael was caught completely off guard, but instinctively removed the hat and shook out her mane of blond hair as she began to sign.

"Me next!" pleaded another, "And can you do one to my brother Simon? He thought you looked really fit on TV last night!"

Soon there were so many children in the queue that the Newskids almost missed the bus. Somehow, they had become overnight celebrities and the smell of success was as surprising as it was sweet; but the mood changed abruptly when they turned into Bridgemont Lane. Three police cars were driving in through the school gates, their blue lights flashing urgently. There were murmurs of speculation. Had there been an accident? A break-in, perhaps? Or had something more serious brought out the law in such force?

Every member of staff was on playground duty directing pupils to the hall where Mr. Aynsley was already on the stage with Jason Steed, his parents and two police officers. Mrs. Steed had been crying and looked deathly pale while Jason seemed childlike and frightened as he sat beside his father who was staring at the floor, tugging at his shirt cuffs. There was complete silence as Mr. Aynsley touched Mrs. Steed reassuringly on the shoulder and rose to address the school.

"I'm afraid we start the day with some very serious news," he began. "Jason Steed's sister, Josie, was reported missing at ten o'clock last night and the police have mounted a search that we hope will bring her safely home."

A murmur of alarm spread through the hall. Missing people were sometimes reported on the news, but no-one in their wildest dreams ever imagined that one of their own school friends might suddenly vanish. Everyone was in shock and some of Josie's classmates were being comforted by teachers as the headmaster continued his address.

"Detective Inspector Webster is in charge of the investigation," he said. "His officers will be speaking to everyone in Josie's year during the course of the day, hoping to gather clues as to why she disappeared and where she might have gone."

Max glanced towards the back of the hall where P.C. Hancock, the Schools Liaison Officer, was handing out class lists to four colleagues.

"This doesn't look good." he whispered to Becky. "I hope she's O.K."

As the day wore on, rumours began to spread that a kidnapper might be somewhere at large and scores of parents had gathered at the school gates when the children came out at half past three. The atmosphere on the bus was sombre as everyone looked out at the posters of Josie that were hanging on lamp posts and in shop windows along the homeward route. Max's heart went out to Jason. They may have had their differences, but he shuddered to think how it must feel not to know whether your own sister is alive or dead.

The evening was subdued in the Taylor household and, exhausted after one disturbed night, Max quickly fell into a deep sleep, only to be jolted awake by the strident ring-tone of his mobile. Without opening his eyes, he stretched across to the bedside table and pulled it to his ear.

"Hello," he mumbled, forcing himself into

consciousness and squinting at the greenish numbers of the digital clock glowing hazily through the darkness. It was eleven thirty.

"Max!" whispered a voice. "It's Jason Steed."

Instantly alert, Max switched on the lamp and felt for his glasses.

"Hi, Jason." he answered quietly, then paused – unsure what to say next. "I'm really sorry about your sister. Is there any news?"

"Nothing. The police are going to drag the river tomorrow – but they won't find her..." There was a long silence. "...Look, I know I've given you grief over the years, and it's stupid pretending I haven't..."

Max sensed that Jason was steeling himself to say something, but seemed reluctant to begin.

"That's not important," he said. "Is there any way I can help? I'll do anything I can..."

Jason hesitated. It was clear that he was holding something back.

"I...I can't talk now," he faltered. "Can you meet me at the bus shelter in ten minutes...?"

Before Max could answer, the line went dead. He pulled on jeans, a thick jumper and an anorak then let himself out into the freezing February night, his breath steaming in the orange glow of the street lights. Jason was at the shelter first. He was wearing only tracksuit bottoms and a tee shirt, but seemed not to notice the cold, even though his teeth were chattering and his skinny arms had turned quite blue.

"Josie won't come back," he said, picking up the conversation as though it hadn't been interrupted. "Not while the police are involved and mum and dad are splashed all over the papers. All the fuss will frighten her away."

"But the appeals might encourage her to make contact," suggested Max. "Then at least you and your family would know that she's safe."

Jason shook his head. "It's not that simple," he said flatly, sitting on a bench and raking his fingers through his unwashed hair. "Dad and Josie have been at each other's throats for ages. She couldn't do anything right in his book. He criticised her clothes, her friends, her manners and just about everything she did. Then he lost his job and started drinking. Sometimes he'd get really aggressive and his moods were tearing the family apart; but I had to be strong for mum's sake…"

There was a catch in his voice, then tears coursed down his cheeks and he began to shake. Suddenly, the behaviour at school began to make sense. With so much trouble and unhappiness at home, it was hardly surprising that Jason found it hard to make friends. Perhaps it was inevitable that he would fall in with a bully like Keith Pratt.

"How are your mum and dad coping?" asked Max.

"They're gutted," Jason replied. "Dad'll do anything to get her back and hasn't touched a drink since she disappeared. I can't believe it's taken something like this to make him realise how much he really loves her; but it'll be hard to convince Josie of that now that she's started a new life."

"What do you mean?" asked Max, suspecting that Jason knew more than he had told the police.

"I'll only say if you swear not to breathe a word to anyone."

Max paused, wondering what would happen if he promised not to pass on what might prove to be vital information; then, seeing the despair in Jason's eyes, he made his decision.

"Alright. I promise."

A look of relief crossed Jason's face and he began to open up.

"She was friendly with a family of travellers. I don't know their names, but they're fairground workers who tour the country telling fortunes. Josie was always talking about them, but she made me promise never to say anything to mum or dad. She spent hours in their caravans and was treated as part of the family. There was even some weird adoption ceremony where she was given a pair of hooped ear-rings and a special Romany name. That's when she started to change. It was as if they had some sort of power over her. She became more and more distant and money started to disappear from mum's purse. The gypsies told her that they were too poor to buy crystals and tarot cards, but Josie wouldn't listen when I tried to tell her that they were just using her to steal from us. In her eyes, they could do no wrong. Then on Monday night, she came home in tears because they were moving on. She seemed to be in some sort of trance and kept repeating something the gypsy woman had said…"

Suddenly, a look of panic flashed in his eyes and he gripped Max's shoulder.

"Please don't let me down, Max," he begged. "If you pass any of this on, we're going to lose her…"

"Take it easy," said Max, gently unlocking his fingers. "What did the woman say?"

"She told Josie that all children are free spirits who can only find true happiness on the road. That was the last time I saw her."

"But that sounds like kidnapping!" said Max. "If these gypsies have abducted her, you *must* tell the police. They've already stolen money from your mum and dad. The next thing could be a ransom note coming through the door – and who knows what might happen to Josie if your parents don't pay up?"

Jason stared at him hard. "No!" he cried. "Any approach from an adult will drive her further away from us. I believe someone nearer her age is more likely to break the spell. That's why I've come to you. I want Newskids on the Net to take up the search. Please help me, Max. we've got to find her before it's too late!"

Chapter 8

THE SEARCH

It snowed hard during the night and the Newskids woke to find text messages asking them to meet at the studio before school. Mrs. Cooper's car wouldn't start, so everyone had to wait for Rachael to make the mile-and-a-half trudge to the Taylors' house before Max would disclose any details of his midnight meeting with Jason.

"How much of this does he want us to k..keep from the police?" asked Becky who had become quite jittery by the time he finished the story.

"They mustn't know about the gypsy connection," he said, "I promised we'd say nothing about that. Jason's convinced that if the police start questioning every travelling community from John O'Groats to Land's End, Josie will be drawn closer and closer to these people. She may never come home."

"But it's the only *clue*!" shrilled Rachael, drying her boots over an electric heater. "If we can't tell our audience that she could be hanging out with a travelling family, the chances of anyone finding her are practically zilch."

The expressions around the room told Max that the others shared her concern, but he tried to remain positive.

"Then perhaps there's a way of *suggesting* where she is without giving it all away,"he said, chewing thoughtfully at the end of a biro from which a faint, blue stain was seeping over his lower lip.

There was a long silence as the team weighed the huge responsibility that rested on their shoulders.

"You do realise that keeping this quiet could land us in big trouble, don't you, Max?" said Becky, who was feeling more and more uneasy about Jason's plan. "And suppose the gypsies *haven't* got Josie's happiness and wellbeing at heart? How are we going to live with ourselves if she's found lying face down in a d..ditch somewhere?"

Max had been awake most of the night agonising over that, and many other, sinister possibilities, but his reply was filled with conviction.

"I saw how desperate and ill Jason looked last night," he said. "I also saw how much he loves his sister. If he's convinced that this is the best way of getting her back, I think we should do as he asks. It's only for a few days. We can post pictures of Josie on the site from now until Wednesday – then he'll make a live appeal on the programme. If that doesn't work, he's promised to go straight to the police."

At that moment, a biting wind blew in and Jason appeared in a flurry of snowflakes. There was an uncomfortable silence.

"I've probably no right to ask you guys to help me after the prize idiot I've been at school," he said quietly. "All I can say is that Josie's the best sister anyone could have and I can't stand seeing my mum and dad suffer any more."

Once Ollie saw the pain etched on the fourteen-year-old's face, memories of the past melted away.

"No worries, Jason," he said, touching him gently on the shoulder. "We'll get her back. All you have to do is keep believing that."

In that instant, the atmosphere lifted and the studio came alive with suggestions and offers of support. Suddenly, Max knew that he had made the right decision and Jason was overwhelmed – he had almost forgotten how good it felt to have friends.

"Have you brought any pictures, Jason?" asked Becky, who was anxious to get started. "The sooner I get them on the home page the better."

Jason handed her a CD and a small bundle of prints. As she spread them across the news desk, a strip of four passport-sized shots caught Max's eye. They had been taken in a booth at the local station and showed Josie looking carefree and relaxed, blond hair cascading over the shoulders of her school blazer. Her face was turned slightly away from the camera showing off one of a pair of large, golden hoped ear-rings.

"Those must be the ones the travellers gave her!" he exclaimed. "Put that strip right across the page, Becky – then visitors to the site might make the gypsy connection for themselves!"

"I wouldn't count on it, Max." she cautioned. "There must be *thousands* of fifteen-year-olds who wear hooped ear-rings – and they don't all live in caravans, you know."

Max knitted his brow, but Rachael had a suggestion.

"I remember something," she said. "Josie helped with make-up for the school play. None of us could talk to her much because she was always listening to some weird C.D.on her iPod. It was called *'Follow Your Soul'* by a band called Free Spirit and the album sleeve was covered with pictures of scruffy-looking people sitting round camp fires wearing bandanas and loads of ethnic jewellery."

"Why don't we buy a copy and post it next to the ear-ring shot?" Ollie chimed in."That would get the message across. I've got a twenty quid H.M.V. voucher left over from my birthday. I was going to check out 'Football Grooves of the Decade', but it's out of stock..."

"Too much detail, Sniff!" said Max, cutting him short. "It's a good idea, though – and I've got the perfect line to go with it:

'HAVE YOU SEEN THE SCHOOLGIRL WITH THE GYPSY IN HER SOUL?'".

Becky quickly scanned the pictures into the P.C. and was just typing in the text when another thought struck her.

"Supposing someone gets in touch claiming to be Josie herself," she asked. "How can we be sure it's really her?"

"That's easy," said Jason. "The gypsies have given her a special name and I'm the only other person who knows what it is. If anyone says they're my sister, ask them what that name is. If the answer is Simsiana, you'll be talking to Josie."

***

By Sunday night, Goston was hidden under a thick, snowy blanket that made the prospect of finding a fifteen-year-old schoolgirl, who could have been anywhere in the country, seem more daunting than ever. Josie's page had been on the site for three days and the Newskids had spent every waking moment taking it in turns to monitor the P.Cs. Max hadn't stopped all weekend. Even off duty he'd been making hot drinks for everyone and giving moral support; but by ten fifteen, he felt ready to drop and took himself off to bed leaving Ollie in charge until close-down at eleven.

It was ten forty-five. Ollie was tired, bored and disappointed that there hadn't been a single lead. He knew he was nearing the end of his shift and the ticking of the studio clock was making him drowsy. He yawned as he thought about his nice, warm bed –then dreams took over and he drifted into goal at Gostonborough United, facing a barrage of penalty kicks from Lenny Dimaggio. The last shot hit him like a ballistic missile and he woke with a start as his head banged painfully against the desk top. For a moment,he wondered where he was, then his eyes lighted on the inbox where a single e-mail was waiting to be read. The subject box contained one short phrase:

I've seen her.

"How long have I been asleep?" he panicked, instantly alert and tugging his hair in frustration. His heart raced as he clicked on the mouse and watched the little white envelope spill its contents across the screen. The message had arrived fifteen minutes earlier and read:

She's in Devon. E-mail straight back. Dad doesn't like me on line at night. Daisy.

Ollie's fingers were trembling as he typed a reply.

Thanks Daisy. Come to the Newskids chat room. Must talk a.s.a.p. Ollie Morris.

He hit 'send' and waited. Seconds became minutes, but there was no answer. His mind was racked with guilt. How would he forgive himself if Daisy had logged off while he'd been asleep – and how would he break the news to Jason? After what seemed an eternity, a wave of relief swept over him as a line of text flowed onto the screen.

Hi Ollie. Can't stay long. Dad thinks I'm in bed. Daisy.

That's cool, Daisy. Where did you see her?

Music shop.

How do you know it was Josie?

Big gold ear-rings, but hair black, not blond.

Ollie hesitated. Was this a false alarm? Then he remembered Josie's make-up skills. Perhaps she had coloured her hair…

Was she alone?

No. Older woman buying her new Free Spirit album. Not my thing. I think they're weird.

Do you know where they went?

Another long wait, then the dialogue ended abruptly.

Dad really cross! Barred from computer. Gotta go.

Ollie gave a cry of anguish and slammed both fists on the desktop as the message froze. His head was bursting with all the questions he hadn't asked: Where was the music shop? What was it called? What else had Daisy overheard?

He waited until eleven fifteen, but there was no further contact. It seemed futile, but he sent one final message before shutting down.

Thanks for your help, Daisy. If you see the girl again, please ask her to contact us. All Newskids are under sixteen and we're on Josie's side. Sleep well. Ollie.

***

Monday morning dawned and the freeze continued. The roads were treacherously icy and, although gritting lorries had been out in force, the journey to school was slippery and slow.

Two hundred miles south west of Goston, gale force winds were pounding the Devonshire coast and icy blizzards whipped through the country lanes outside Barnstaple. The pupils of Sandmore Senior School arrived to find that their heating had failed and classes were cancelled for the day. Daisy Stokes and two classmates were in high spirits as they made their way home, pausing to make snowballs and jump into drifts that came up to their knees. Suddenly, a battered truck droned towards them with headlights ablaze. The children scattered as it slewed across the road, missing them by inches and turning onto a small track.

"Lunatic!" shouted Daisy, picking herself up and brushing snow from her school coat. The driver's recklessness had made her suspicious and she peered over the hedge, watching the truck slide to a halt in the middle of a field where a group of caravans seemed to be huddling together for warmth. The embers of a camp fire glowing through the mist reminded her of the pictures on the Newskids website; then she remembered Ollie and imagined how frustrated he must have felt when she'd cut their conversation short. The least she could do was find out who these strangers were and what had brought them to her village.

"You two go ahead!" she said to the others. "I'll catch you up!"

As her friends walked on, Daisy squeezed through a gap in the hedgerow and trudged through the deep snow towards two large trailers parked side by side at the edge of the compound. She wanted to explore, but something told her that visitors might not be welcome in this camp. The curtains of the first caravan were drawn and condensation inside the windows told her that its occupants were still asleep. She was about to inspect the second when a tall woman, dressed all in black, appeared eerily through the swirling snowflakes, carrying two steaming mugs of tea. Daisy darted out of sight between the two trailers, her pulse quickening as the footsteps came closer; then the second caravan swayed as the woman mounted the steps and opened the door.

"Something to warm you up before we begin, my dear," she murmured to someone inside. "As I told you last night..." The door closed and Daisy pressed her ear to the wall, straining to hear what was being said: "...Today, we are going to explore the mysteries of the Tarot..."

The schoolgirl stifled a gasp. The last time she had heard that voice, it was haggling over the price of the new Free Spirit album in CeeDees Music Shop in Barnstaple High Street. Then came the stark realisation that she might be inches away from Josie Steed, the subject of a nationwide missing person search. Standing on tiptoe, she peered nervously through a chink in the curtain, hoping for a glimpse of the second individual who was certainly female, but had her back to the window.

"...This card is The Fool," the gypsy's voice continued. "He is innocently setting out on a journey with no thought for what might be encountered along the way..."

Daisy hardly dared breathe. She knew that, if Josie Steed *was* in the caravan, she could be in danger herself if the fortune-teller saw her. For five long minutes, she stood completely still; then, at last, the other figure leaned forward, tossing back a tangle of long, dark hair as she drew a mug of tea to her lips. In that fleeting moment, Daisy glimpsed the profile of a pale young woman, a heavy golden hoop hanging from each ear. But was it Josie? This person seemed older than the girl on the Newskids site and,to be certain, the schoolgirl knew that she would have to find a way of talking to her alone.

Buttoning her overcoat, Daisy crawled under the caravan and hid herself in the freezing snow. For over an hour, she lay as quiet as a mouse watching the legs of the other gypsies moving back and forth as they went about their business. Then, when every muscle in her body was aching with cold, there was a hollow, scratching sound overhead. Someone was raking out the ashes from a log stove. Suddenly, the caravan moved again as the older woman rose to open the door.

"I'm feeling the chill," she said, stepping out onto a narrow platform at the top of a short, rickety staircase. "Make friends with the cards while I fetch some more wood for the fire."

Daisy held her breath as the gypsy's boots clumped heavily down the wooden treads, inches away from her face. She waited for her to disappear into the trees then, dusting the snow from her clothes, climbed the steps and tapped at the flaking paintwork on the caravan door. A net curtain moved slightly, then it opened an inch or two and a pair of timid, blue eyes stared out of the darkness.

"Hi! My name's Daisy Stokes," she whispered, taking an uneasy glance over her shoulder. "May I come in? It's really cold out here."

The young gypsy ushered her inside and offered a stool. Daisy paused for a moment,hoping they would strike up some sort of conversation, but the girl didn't speak.

"Look, I know this is none of my business," she continued, "And I haven't come to pry; but if your name is Josie Steed, I have a message from your brother Jason..."

The girl sank silently onto the window seat and stared back.

"...He's seriously worried about you and wants to know you're O.K."

There was still no answer. Daisy peeped out of the window and saw the gypsy woman making her way back across the compound. She felt scared now and was desperately trying to think of some way of getting this person to talk.

"Look, I daren't stay much longer," she breathed, "Jason has some mates who run a website called Newskids on the Net. All of them are under sixteen and have no connection with any organisation like the police. They're spending every spare minute waiting for you to get in touch..."

Suddenly, a loud clattering brought her to her feet. The woman was on her knees in the snow, cursing as she retrieved an armful of dropped firewood. Still without a word, the girl tugged at Daisy's sleeve and led her down the steps at the back of the caravan. Their eyes met for an instant, but her expression was as inscrutable as ever.

"Please go to the cybercafé in town," urged Daisy. "It's called Surfers' Paradise. Remember: Newskids on the Net!" Then she turned and was quickly lost in the thickening snowfall.

★★★

The atmosphere at Bridgemont was cheerless in the wake of Josie's disappearance. The radiators were on full power, but nevertheless a gloomy chill pervaded the school as pupils went about their Monday routine. Max paid the price for a virtually sleepless weekend by being half an hour late for registration and collecting a detention for failing to hand in his Geography homework. The others fared little better. Rachael forgot her lines in the middle of a Theatre

Studies prepared piece, Becky was told off for being inattentive in I.T. and Ollie flunked a science test because he was still racked with guilt for losing their only lead in the search for Josie Steed. All in all, it was not a good day and the Newskids were longing for school to end so that they could get back to the studio.

Becky went home with Max. Her mother was going out for the evening and had arranged to pick her up from the Taylors' at half past ten. Mrs. Roberts had given strict instructions that she was to get down to her homework and stay indoors; but French grammar was the last thing on Becky's mind as she and Max made a dash for the shed without even saying hello to his parents.

"Hey! I want a word with you two!" called Mr. Taylor from his study window.

"What is it, dad?" replied Max, struggling to get the key into the padlock while Becky scraped an inch or two of frost from a window pane and peered hopefully inside at the P.C.

"I think the three of us need to talk. Would you mind stopping whatever it is you're doing and coming inside, please?"

Max had just managed to open the door when the request was repeated with more force.

"*Now*, please!"

The teenagers hurried back to the house, bracing themselves for a ticking off for the amount of time they had spent in the studio over the previous four days; but it was soon clear that Max's parents were more than just annoyed – they were seriously concerned.

"You had all weekend to finish that rain forest project, Max," said Mr. Taylor sternly, "And it was due in this morning, wasn't it?" Max took a breath, but was not given time to answer. "Mum found the folder hidden under your duvet. You didn't even look at it,did you?"

"I'm sorry, dad…It's been difficult, you see…Newskids has one or two major projects on the go at the moment, and I…"

"I don't want excuses," snapped his father, "When mum and I agreed to letting you have the shed, it was on condition that Newskids on the Net didn't get in the way of school work. You agreed to that – and now you're going back on your word."

"But dad…"

"No 'buts', Max! No-one, least of all me, is saying that the TV station isn't a great idea; but it's a hobby – and hobbies have to take second place when it comes to getting decent grades."

Nick Taylor paused and dropped into his swivel chair.

"Just look at yourselves," he sighed. "You're like a pair of zombies with those dark circles under your eyes. I'm not surprised you missed the bus this morning, Max – and your mum's just as concerned about this as we are, Becky."

The teenagers stared at the carpet as Mr. Taylor came to his point.

"That's why I'm forbidding you from going anywhere near that shed until after school on Wednesday. Is that clear?"

Waves of panic surged through Max's brain. He had already put Josie's safety at risk by gambling that

Newskids on the Net could bring her home. Two lost days could leave their efforts in tatters and set the police investigation still further back.

"Please, dad...we must have more time," he pleaded. "You've got to believe me. This is important... really important."

Mr. Taylor sensed the conflict raging inside his son and wanted to understand the cause.

"But you haven't told me what the 'this' is, Max!" he cried in exasperation. "I'll give you one last chance, and I want a straight answer: what has been keeping you kids in that shed all hours of the day and night for the last four days?"

Max had never lied to his parents and knew that his father was trying to give him the benefit of the doubt; but he couldn't tell the truth without breaking his promise to Jason. Becky knew that her best friend was on the horns of a terrible dilemma and was searching for a way of preventing him from deceiving his father without destroying their plan.

"It's J..Josie Steed," she stammered, deciding that there was no alternative other than to reveal part of the secret. "Her brother Jason thinks she may be too scared to contact the p..police, so he asked us to post an appeal on the site. We've been monitoring the P.C. all weekend, hoping she'll get in touch..."

"And...?"

Becky hesitated.

"Come on, Becky," Mr. Taylor pressed her. "There's something you're not telling me. Has Josie Steed been in contact with Newskids on the Net?"

"No."

Her reply was emphatic and, to Max's great relief, Mr. Taylor let the matter drop.

"Then you can check your e-mails before school tomorrow," he concluded. "Everyone in the country is looking for Josie Steed – and if anyone knows where she is, they'll contact the police or the Missing People Helpline. I'm delighted you kids are getting behind the search, but the responsibility lies with the authorities – not Newskids on the Net."

The children felt utterly defeated as they sat in the kitchen and tried to get on with their homework. Mr. Taylor had left the study door open, making it impossible for them to talk without being overheard; so Becky began to revise French irregular verbs while Max rummaged through his case for Chesterton's Companion to the Shakespeare Tragedies. Suddenly, his hand brushed against his mobile phone and Becky raised a questioning eyebrow as he pulled it out and, raising a finger to his lips, began to compose a text.

Sniff. Becky and I barred from shed. No-one to check e-mails. Any chance of taking over till 10-ish? No lights. Key under mat. Don't reply. M.

Removing his shoes, he tiptoed to the front door, eased it open an inch or two and planted the key. Then he slipped back to the kitchen and turned his thoughts to Hamlet's encounter with his father's ghost on the battlements of Elsinore Castle.

***

By ten o'clock, Max and Becky could hardly keep their eyes open. "You go on up to bed," she said. "I'll be fine watching TV until mum gets here. Let's see what tomorrow brings."

Max climbed the stairs and gazed through the landing window, hoping that Ollie was on duty in the unlit shed; then the pressure of the last four days got the better of him and he crashed out on his bed.

Watching Mrs. Steed make another emotional appeal for Josie on the Ten O'clock News was too much for Becky. Her conscience told her that, in spite of Mr. Taylor's ultimatum, she would *have* to pay a final visit to the studio. Suddenly, she thought of the perfect excuse and walked calmly into his study.

"Do you mind if I make one really quick trip to the shed, Mr. T?" she begged. "It's a complete tip down there with all the cups and p..pizza boxes left over from the weekend. The bin men come at seven in the morning. If I bag everything up, we'll save ourselves a load of time and hassle before the show on Wednesday."

Mr. Taylor checked his watch.

"Well, your mum's coming soon," he said. "I suppose a few minutes won't hurt. Off you go – but don't be too long!"

Grabbing a tea tray and a handful of bin liners, Becky ran to the end of the garden. The shed door gave to her touch and she went inside, finding Ollie slumped in a chair, staring disconsolately at the computer screen.

"Any luck, Sniff?"

There was no answer; just a slow shake of the head.

"Time to go home," she said gently, collecting the dirty mugs. "Tomorrow's another day. Max will check the messages again before school."

Tired and dispirited, Ollie followed her up to the house and waited outside while she took the tray into the kitchen.

"You mustn't blame yourself," she whispered, returning to give him a goodnight hug. "Any one of us could have been a few minutes late opening Daisy's message."

Ollie smiled weakly then, carrying his bike to the road to avoid unnecessary noise,he headed for home while Becky returned to the studio to bag up the empty pizza boxes. The cold nipped her fingers as she locked up and was half way back to the house when she remembered that no-one had turned off the P.C.

"Blast!" she hissed, dashing back to the shed and fumbling to get the tiny silver key into the lock. The door swung open and she hurried across the rough, wooden floor. Then she saw it: a single e-mail had arrived in the previously empty inbox. Breathlessly, she clicked on the mouse. There was a momentary flicker and a message exploded across the screen:

Where's Jason?

Becky's hands were shaking as she typed in a reply.

Not here just now. Can we talk in the chat room? I'll be much easier.

Several minutes passed. The computer hummed faintly through the silence, stretching her nerves to breaking point; then she felt a rush of adrenaline as three words cut through the flickering blankness.

Who are you?

My name's Becky Roberts I'm in year ten at Bridgemont School in Goston. Please tell me yours.

Josie.

Becky caught her breath. She was alone now and knew that everything would depend on how she handled this.

Hi Josie! How are you?

Scared. Just seen my picture on the news. Trouble…

Becky's heart was pounding. She had to reassure Josie, but was struggling to find the right words.

You're not in any trouble, Josie. Your family really loves you and wants you back. Your dad would give anything to make things up and Jason misses you so much that it's making him ill.

Can I talk to him?

He'll be here in our studio at seven o'clock tomorrow night.

What studio? What is Newskids on the Net?

It's a children's news station. We do a live webcast every Wednesday from Max Taylor's shed in Goss Street.

As she waited for a response, Becky heard Mr. Taylor calling down from the kitchen.Her mother had arrived.

"Please stay on line…please, please stay…" she murmured, tears of frustration welling in her eyes. Then her body tensed as two short statements ended the exchange.

Gotta go now. They'll be waiting.

Suddenly, Becky remembered that there was something she needed to ask: a single question that would prove beyond doubt that this really was Josie Steed. The keyboard rattled as she made one final effort to catch the girl's attention.

Please don't go yet! Jason told us that you have a special gypsy name. We're dying to know what it is…

There was a seemingly endless pause, but at last she got the answer she wanted.

Simsiana.

Chapter 9

HITTING THE HEADLINES

Becky's mouth was dry as she began the one minute countdown to Wednesday's programme. There had been no further contact from Josie and Max was briefing six of her closest friends who had agreed to lend their voices to the appeal. The Newskids knew that this was their last chance and that, if they failed, the consequences of holding information back from the police could prove very grave indeed.

"Good evening and welcome to Newskids on the Net," Rachael began as the studio went live to thousands of viewers across the nation. "Tonight, we're appealing on behalf of our friend Josie Steed who disappeared from her home in Goston exactly seven days ago."

Jason sat grimly beside her, wiping sweat from his palms as he realised that his family's hopes, and perhaps his sister's life, were riding on a single webcast from a modest shed at the bottom of a school friend's garden.

"If you're watching, Josie, everyone is praying that

you'll find the courage to come home," she continued. "Some of your best mates have messages for you tonight – but first your brother Jason wants to say 'hi'..."

As the camera swung towards him, Jason was powerfully aware that, somewhere beyond its tiny lens, the person he loved most in all the world might be watching at that moment. The thought overwhelmed him and he froze. Rachael knew that, without his contribution, the appeal was doomed to failure yet, in spite of all her coaxing and encouragement, he remained tongue-tied. Every second of silence seemed like an hour and Becky sensed the programme spiralling out of control. She knew that, regardless of her stammer, she would have to step in.

"Even if I do stammer, I can still say what I need to say," she told herself, thinking back to her speech therapy sessions in the fifth year as she stepped onto the set and knelt calmly at Jason's side.

"I know how hard this for you," she whispered, giving his hand a reassuring squeeze. "Just try to forget that it's a t..television programme and concentrate on talking to Rachael..."

Jason sat motionless, staring blankly at the desk top.

"...Tell her how your life has changed since Josie left, just as we planned. Remember, we want her back as much as you do. We're a team. You're not on your own any more."

Very slowly, he lifted his gaze to Rachael and, once they had eye contact, began to speak – his voice faltering at first, but quickly gaining strength.

"They say you don't appreciate how precious

something is until you lose it," he said softly. "That's the way my family feels about Josie, especially dad..."

Soon he was talking about his sister with such feeling and understanding that Becky was close to tears as she slipped quietly back to her place at the P.C.

For nearly an hour, Josie's friends and classmates did all they could to persuade her to come forward; but, as the programme drew to a close, there had still been no word and Jason faced the heartbreaking truth that nothing short a miracle was going to bring his sister back.

"If you're watching, Josie, *please* get in touch," pleaded Rachael as a tall, slender girl carrying an acoustic guitar joined her at the news desk. "We're into the last five minutes of the programme and it's time to bring on your best friend, Anna Murphy."

"Hi, Josie!" said Anna, smiling into the webcam and strumming a sequence of minor chords. "Remember the songs we wrote together? You always had a great way with words. This was our favourite. We called it 'Spirit High'."

Anna closed her eyes and was about to sing when the mood was shattered by a sudden rapping at the shed door. Max sprang to his feet, furious that someone had intruded on a moment that might have moved Josie to make contact. The knocking became more insistent and Ollie swung the camera towards the door as his friend flung it open and stared outside at a mysterious figure dressed in a long black overcoat, the shoulders dusted with snow. There was a scarf tied tightly around the mouth and chin and the forehead glistened with water trickling from a mop of soaking hair. While Max led the stranger inside, Anna continued the song. Her performance lent the words great power because they came straight from the heart.

"When precious little hope remains,
Your body trapped, your soul in chains..."

Suddenly, the unknown visitor began to join in, singing in perfect harmony and seeming to know every word...

"...No-one ever can deny
That freedom makes the spirit fly..."

Very slowly, Jason rose to his feet. He inched forward, reaching gingerly towards the scarf as he summoned up the courage to uncover the face. The stranger showed no resistance as he pulled it away, then cried with joy. The miracle had happened. Josie was home! The television pictures spoke a thousand words as brother and sister clung to each other as if to stop anyone or anything from parting them again; then the whole studio erupted with everyone clapping, cheering and punching the air in delight.

"I just don't know what to say!" cried an ecstatic Jason, turning to Ollie's camera which was still live. "Newskids on the Net...and all the online fans...we'll never be able to thank you enough...!"

"Especially Daisy in Barnstaple," added Josie, hugging her brother and laughing and crying at the same time. "I hardly know you, Daisy, but if you hadn't done what you did, I wouldn't be here now!"

When the programme ended, torch beams danced across the garden as Jason and Josie, beside themselves with happiness, followed the Newskids up to the kitchen where Max's parents were also dewy-eyed with emotion – and more than a little pride.

"It's wonderful to see you, Josie!" said Mrs. Taylor, draping her overcoat over the radiator and handing her a mug of hot cocoa. "You're soaked to the skin. Wherever have you been?"

"It's a long story," replied the fifteen-year-old, cupping the mug in her hands as Jason gently rubbed her shoulders. "But I'd probably still be there if Newskids on the Net hadn't taught me that love of family and friends is the greatest power of all."

"How did you get back?" asked Becky.

"Once we'd made contact, I decided to escape while the gypsies were asleep. It was a four mile walk to the station and by the time I got there I thought I'd die of cold; so I took this overcoat from a cardboard box in the doorway of a charity shop. I didn't have a penny, but the trains weren't running in any case. Eventually, I managed to hitch a lift on a pottery truck heading north east and somehow found my way back to Goston." Then she hugged her brother again, sobbing: "I'm so sorry for what I've put you through. It's so good to be back!"

"I'll run you kids straight home," insisted Mr. Taylor, leading them out into the hallway. "We don't want you catching pneumonia, Josie."

Grabbing the car keys from their hook on the wall, he opened the front door; but no sooner had they stepped out onto the porch than a battery of lights blazed into their eyes and pandemonium broke out. Every newspaper and television station in the country had picked up on the Newskids' webcast and the street was under siege from reporters and cameramen sent to cover the story.

"Hugh Jeffries, Daily Express!" called a voice as flash guns exploded from all directions. "Are Josie and Jason prepared to make any comment at this time?"

"Cliff Elliott, Sky News!" cried another as his colleague held a camera inches from Josie's face. "What is Newskids on the Net and how did it find you?"

Then everyone started to shout at once and the bewildered runaway clung to Jason's arm, using her free hand to shield her eyes from the glare.

"Give them space, please!" called Mr. Taylor, forcing a path through the crowd. "I'm sure the Steed family will talk to you soon, but I must get these kids home."

But the reporters were undeterred.

"Vic Masters, Sunday People!" yelled another. "Where have you been for the last seven days, Josie?"

Before she could answer, Nick Taylor had bundled the two children into his V.W. Beetle and was speeding away with photographers sprinting alongside, snatching any pictures they could through the misty windows.

With Josie gone, the commotion quickly subsided and the street was returning to normal when a reporter from The Sun spotted Rachael.

"Excuse me, love!" he called, "You're the presenter of Newskids on the Net, aren't you?"

Sensing another angle on the story, a dozen or more photographers came racing back. Rachael looked startled, but remembered to check her hair before they went to work.

"It was a team effort, guys," she explained, striking a pose as cameras flashed and clattered around her. "I'd like you to meet my editor, Max Taylor, our ace cameraman Ollie Morris – and this is Becky Roberts who designed the site..." In the time it took for the others to join her on the doorstep, the television crews had also returned and before long the Newskids were being paraded in Max's front garden like film stars at an Oscars ceremony giving one interview after another until the reporters ran out of questions and the cameramen ran out of film. Fifteen minutes later,Goss Street was deserted again.

★★★

Max woke to a bleak and drizzly morning, wondering if the night's events had been anything more than a dream; but any doubts were dispelled when his mother rushed into his bedroom.

"Quick, Max!" she called. "You're on Breakfast News!"

Racing down to the kitchen, he found his father glued to the TV watching him explaining how Newskids on the Net used its network of viewers to get Josie back. They zapped to ITV where Ollie and Sparks were regaling a "Daybreak" reporter with the story of how Daisy got in touch, then over to Sky News where Becky was talking about Josie's gypsy name.

"You kids have certainly made an impact!" said Mr. Taylor, pointing to the bundle of newspapers he had just collected from the corner shop. Max was gobsmacked by the headlines: '*NEWSKIDS FIND MISSING SCHOOLGIRL*' proclaimed The Daily Telegraph; '*NEWSKIDS RIGHT ON LINE!*' declared the Mail while The Sun carried a picture of Rachael standing alluringly on the doorstep with the caption '*STUNNING NEWS! GOSTON KIDS FIND JOSIE!*'

The reality was slowly sinking in. Not only had Newskids on the Net webcast the story of the week, they *were* the story of the week. There was only one problem: where could they go from here?

Chapter 10

A MAN CALLED SMITH

The weekend felt very flat. Nothing seemed to be happening in Goston and the pressure was on to find stories for next Wednesday's programme. The Newskids knew that their audience would be expecting something more exciting than a skateboarding hamster after last week's triumph and Max had called an emergency meeting on Monday after school.

Everyone was scouring the local papers for ideas while Ollie lay flat out on the news desk, listening to Radio Goston on his headphones. Suddenly, he sat bolt upright, almost strangling himself with the leads.

"It's confirmed!" he shouted. "Lenny Dimaggio has signed! He plays his first match for United next Saturday! It's the local derby against Killerton!"

"There's our lead story!" cried Max, grabbing the headphones and listening in to the rest of the report.

"But every TV station in the country will be after him," said Rachael dismissively. "What makes you think Dimaggio will give an interview to a bunch of kids?"

Max bridled at this. He was proud that Newskids on the Net had found Josie Steed and felt sure that

Gostonborough United would take them seriously enough to consider their request.

"I'll bet you any money you like that I can talk them into it," he challenged her, leafing determinedly through the phone book.

"Done!" she accepted. "A fiver says you won't pull it off."

The rest of the team waited with bated breath while Max called Gostonborough's headquarters but, two minutes later, the number was still ringing and he had to assume that the offices had closed for the day. It seemed pointless holding on, yet something told him to be patient. He firmly believed that their new-found celebrity might open doors that would otherwise have remained closed. Seconds later, the switchboard picked up, catching him completely off guard.

"Gostonborough United."

"Oh!...er...Hi!...This is Max Taylor...from Newskids on the Net," he faltered, "That's right, we're the ones who found the missing girl...Yes, we were on the news...The one with the glasses?...Yeah, that was me...Good of you to say so...!"

He glanced at Rachael. "Just a bunch of kids, eh?" he thought, feeling more confident as he came to the point of his call.

"...I'm ringing to offer Lenny Dimaggio the star interview spot in next Wednesday's show...Yes, I'll hold on..." There was a pause while the call was transferred. "They're putting me through to Diana Sheldon in the Press Office," he whispered to the others. "Fingers crossed!"

Everyone was on tenterhooks as Diana picked up

and Max made his pitch, pressing politely for a quick decision.

"...Any chance of calling me later today?' he asked, "...No, I'm afraid not. We can't keep the spot open till then...You will?...Oh, that would be wicked!...Thanks a lot... Cheers."

There was a murmur of excitement.

"You've got more cheek than a pair of builder's jeans!" laughed Ollie. "What did she say?"

"I think we're in with a shout," he said quietly, not wanting to seem too optimistic in case the whole thing fell through. "She's going to check his schedule and call me back."

The prospect of getting an interview with an international soccer star made everything else seem pretty tame. There was a small flurry of excitement when Sparks discovered that the local Beavers had unearthed a valuable Roman sandal on Penfold Flats – but the story collapsed when it turned out to be one of a pair of discarded Marks and Spencer sling-backs. By seven o'clock, everyone was desperate for the phone to ring – but it was looking less and less likely that the Dimaggio interview would come off.

"You were probably right, Rachael," said Max, conceding defeat. "Why should he give an interview to Newskids on the Net when every newspaper and TV station in the country is after him? Looks like we'll have to get the skateboarding hamster after all."

Becky was reaching for the video-phone when its piercing ring tone sounded and she pulled her hand back in shock.

"Newskids on the Net!" said Max, grabbing it

before the end of the first note. His eyes widened as the caller gave her name. "Hi, Diana…Thanks for getting back to me…" He looked across at Becky who held up two pairs of tightly-crossed fingers. "…O.K.…I'll just check that my cameraman is available…" Covering the mouthpiece,he turned to Ollie, grinning from ear to ear. "You'd better be available, Sniff! We're only interviewing Lenny Dimaggio before his training session at four thirty tomorrow!"

Everyone shrieked with delight – and Rachael handed over the fiver.

★★★

Floodlights blazed into the night sky as Max and Ollie cycled towards Gostonborough United's training ground. Dimaggio's first work-out with the team had drawn a sizeable crowd including some hard-bitten faces from out of town who showed allegiance to their hero by wearing chunky metal rings in any parts of their bodies that would take a piercing.

"Hold up, you two!" shouted the security man as the boys skidded to a halt by the car park barrier. "You can't go any further unless you're on my list!"

"Max Taylor and Ollie Morris from Newskids on the Net," panted Max, adding with relish: "We're here to interview Lenny Dimaggio."

The grumpy man scanned a piece of paper and scowled back at them, jerking his thumb in the direction of the main entrance.

"You can park your bikes outside," he said. "Wait in the lobby. Diana will come and fetch you."

Diana Sheldon was a bright P.R. executive in her mid-twenties. She wore a smart, navy trouser suit and her shiny brown hair was cut in a fashionable bob.

"Hi! You must be Max and Ollie," she smiled. "Sorry I couldn't invite your friends,but Lenny's got quite a full schedule today. Some other time, maybe."

The boys were beginning to feel quite nervous about interviewing one of the biggest names in world football but, before they could reply, there was a loud guffaw and two men carrying sports bags came in through the revolving doors. Ollie's stomach tingled as he recognised Dave Ingram, the Gostonborough goalkeeper talking to midfielder Graham Hackett. They were sharing some juicy gossip about a certain Manchester United player when Ingram spotted Diana and came over to them.

"And how's my favourite P.R. girl, then?" he grinned, planting a kiss on both her cheeks. "I've put on a clean shirt today. Must make a good impression on the great Mr. Dimaggio – *if* he turns up!"

Diana looked alarmed.

"What do you mean 'if he turns up'?"

"Let's just say he was slightly the worse for wear last night," said Hackett, joining the group. "I'm told he was knocking back vodka shots at The Speakeasy Club till four in the morning, then tried to pick a fight with the barman. They had to throw him out. I expect he's nursing a monumental hangover, so goodness knows if he'll be in any fit state for training tonight."

There were a lot of questions Diana wanted to ask but, remembering that Max and Ollie were there as members of the Press, she quickly changed the subject.

"Erm...I'd like you guys to meet Max Taylor and Ollie Morris from Newskids on the Net," she said. "They've come to interview Lenny before the session."

"Nice to meet you, kids!" said the goalkeeper, shaking their hands. "Just give him plenty of black coffee and he'll be as good as gold. Hope it goes well for you!"

There were more howls of laughter as the two players disappeared towards the changing rooms and Diana turned her attention to the boys.

"I've allocated one of our physio rooms for your filming," she explained, checking her watch. "It's in the basement, so it should be nice and quiet. Will that be alright?"

"Sounds brilliant," said Max, "How much time will we have for the interview...?"

Before she could answer, the P.R. girl was distracted by an older man barging into the lobby carrying a large leather brief case. He was powerfully built and obviously in a hurry. His craggy face reminded Max of a boxer who had spent too many bruising years in the ring and he wore so much expensive jewellery that his hands looked like prizes in a penny arcade.

"May I help?" she asked politely.

The man swaggered towards them. There was an intimidating air about him and, as he moved into the light, the boys noticed that part of his right ear was missing.

"Dimaggio's expecting me," he growled. "Where is he?"

"Are you from the Press?"

"What's it to you?"

"I'm the club's Public Relations Manager. My name's Diana Sheldon. May I know yours?"

"Smith will do. Just call me Smith."

Diana found the man's attitude offensive and answered more coolly.

"I'm afraid he's running late, Mr. Smith. Perhaps you'd be kind enough to wait here while I look after these children."

Smith gave a bad-tempered sigh and sat heavily on a leather-backed chair, looking impatiently at his gold Rolex.

The boys were getting anxious as Diana led them downstairs. Training was due to start in twenty minutes and, if Lenny didn't arrive soon, there would be no time left for the interview.

"Don't worry," she said, unlocking the physio room. "I'm sure he won't be much longer."

The door swung open, releasing a faint smell of embrocation, then her mobile rang.

"Hello. Diana Sheldon…"

The P.R. girl motioned for them to go inside while she took the call. It was a large,sparsely furnished room containing treatment beds, storage cupboards and a human skeleton hanging on a tall metal stand. The only link to the outside world was a run of very high basement windows looking out onto the car park. Ollie quickly decided to film Dimaggio with the lights off, using a single angle-poise lamp to cast his shadow on the wall and make him look really dramatic. All they needed now was for the superstar to arrive.

"We have a problem, I'm afraid," sighed Diana, ending the call. "Lenny's been delayed. If the worst comes to the worst, I'll try to persuade him to stay on after training, but I can't guarantee it – and there are four other journalists in the queue. Would you mind waiting here? I have to go back to the office and break the news to The Daily Express. I'll keep you posted."

Then she was gone.

Ollie set up his camera and turned off the lights, saving the angle-poise until Dimaggio arrived; but at a quarter to five, they were still sitting in darkness, listening to the muffled sound of shouts and thudding footballs as the training session got underway.

"I'd better call the others," said Max gloomily. "They'll have to start looking for something else to put in the show tomorrow..."

But Ollie wasn't listening. The roar of a high-performance engine had drawn him to his feet.

"That's the Aston!" he cried, clambering onto a table and peering up through one of the high windows. "I'd recognise it anywhere!"

Max leaped to his side as a pair of headlights swept into the car park and the number-plate LD9 nosed into the space directly overhead. The headlights died and the striker emerged; but instead of making straight for the dressing room, he slouched against the bonnet as though he were waiting for someone. Suddenly, in the faint glow that spilled from the pitch, they noticed another man moving quickly across the tarmac. Dimaggio gave an impatient wave and the figure broke into a run, arriving breathlessly at the car. The two men kept their voices low making it impossible to hear the conversation through the double glazed windows; but there was no mistaking the identity of the second person: it was Smith. After a minute or so, he stooped to open the briefcase and uttered one sentence that the boys could faintly discern:

"I want to phone Gold in the second half..."

It meant absolutely nothing to them, but it certainly did to Dimaggio who nodded as Smith handed over a large, padded envelope; then the two men separated and the striker sprinted off to change for what remained of the training session.

"What was all that about?" wondered Ollie. "Who's 'Gold' – and why should Smith want to phone him in the second half?"

"To be honest, I couldn't care less," grumbled Max. "Our viewers are expecting Dimaggio's interview as the main item in tomorrow's show. What are we going to tell them if he blows us out?"

Their worst fears were confirmed when Diana returned. She was a good deal less composed now and her red, slightly swollen eyes told them that she had been crying.

"Sorry, guys," she said, "I did my best, but he's cancelled all interviews for today."

"But he *can't*!" protested Ollie. "We're relying on him for tomorrow night's programme! There must be *something* you can do!"

"The Mirror and The Daily Star were relying on him for tomorrow morning's sports pages." she sighed, "My hands are tied, I'm afraid."

The boys looked completely gutted and, although

she was shaken and upset, Diana was already thinking of how she could make it up to them.

"How about interviewing me for your programme?" she suggested. "I'm no Lenny Dimaggio, but I know a lot about Saturday's game. Perhaps your audience would be happy with a stand in until you can get the real thing."

The boys rated Diana. Someone had obviously given her a hard time, yet she remained friendly and professional, even offering a solution to their problem; so Ollie moved the camera over to a 'Go! Go! Gostonboro'!' poster where Max asked her to preview the match.

"Normally, I would expect a close game against Killerton," she predicted. "But they're carrying some injuries at the moment and, with Dimaggio on board, we're quietly confident."

"I understand he missed some training tonight," probed Max, seeing no reason why the striker should be let off scott-free, "The fans may not see that as a great start to a career with a new club – especially just before a local derby."

"Lenny Dimaggio is a team player," said the P.R. girl protectively. "The media loves to talk about unprofessional conduct because it makes for good headlines; but Lenny's footballing skills will do the talking on Saturday – and the bookmakers make United favourites to win!"

Ollie and Max felt better after the interview – and better still when Diana took them on a tour of the training camp. It was brilliant to see the gym, the dressing rooms – even the laundry where kit was cleaned and pressed after every game. Last of all, they found themselves in a small corridor that led to some storage areas and a small meeting room.Its door was ajar and the light was on.

"What goes on in there?" asked Ollie.

"We call that *Len's Den*," Diana replied. "Dimaggio insisted on having somewhere to use as an office until his new house is ready. The door's open. I don't suppose he'll mind if I sneak you a look inside."

It was a plain, bright room with a washbasin and small desk littered with fan mail and piles of photographs. A tall wardrobe stood against the wall and an expensive suit had been carelessly discarded over a two-seater settee.

Suddenly, the tannoy blared into life.

"Diana Taylor to the Press Office immediately please! Diana Taylor to the Press Office!"

"Oh, no!' she groaned. "Welcome back to the afternoon from hell! That'll be Sky Sport after my blood! I'll have to desert you again, I'm afraid. Back in five minutes!"

It wasn't every day that the boys found themselves alone in the office of an England superstar and they wondered what to do until Diana returned. It was tempting to see what soccer legends kept in the pockets of their Armani suits but, seeing a football balanced on top of a waste paper basket, they settled for heading practice. Ollie had far better ball sense than Max and managed to return every shot until a high lob knocked him off balance and sent him crashing into the wardrobe which completely overturned.

"You *idiot*!" gasped Max, looking in horror at Dimaggio's clothes, shaving kit and other personal effects scattered across the floor. "You'd better help me put this stuff away before she comes back!"

It was the work of seconds to right the wardrobe but, as they manoeuvred it back into position, something far more intriguing than socks, loose change and aftershave came to light: hidden underneath was the padded envelope Smith had handed over in the car park. Some of its contents had spilled onto the carpet and the boys were staring at bundles of fifty pound notes.

"I don't believe this!" gasped Max, peering inside, "There must be a quarter of a million quid here. What's he doing with that sort of cash?"

"Don't ask me," shrugged Ollie, hearing footsteps entering the corridor, "But now's not the time to have a debate about it."

Max stuffed the wads of bank notes back into the envelope and returned it to its hiding place while Ollie frantically refilled the rails and shelves, closing the double doors just as Diana reappeared.

"I'm sorry about tonight," she said, looking slightly askance at the boys who were standing awkwardly in front of the wardrobe like a pair of sentries at attention. "But the good news is that I can offer you another slot at the same time next week."

Max and Ollie were still reeling from their shock, but it was a relief to know that the chance of an interview was still there; and there was even better news to come.

"I have a consolation prize for you," she smiled,

handing them a small white envelope. "I thought these might come in handy – only if you're both free on Saturday afternoon, of course."

Ollie's face lit up as he thumbed it open.

"Qua-li-ty!!" he cried, finding two complimentary tickets to the match. "We've just cancelled all engagements! Thanks, Diana! Go! Go! Gostonboro'!"

Chapter 11

ACTION REPLAY

"I hope you guys will spare a thought for the workers while you're larging it in up the posh seats!" teased Becky as Ollie slung the camcorder over his shoulder. Kick-off was at two thirty and the boys were wearing yellow and green Gostonborough United scarves with matching bobble hats, making the others feel like Cinderellas who hadn't been invited to the ball.

Max felt bad that the rest of the gang couldn't come, but the match was a sell-out and Diana had run out of press tickets.

"Tell you what!" he suggested. "Let's meet up tonight and watch the highlights on "Match of the Day". I'll get the pizzas!"

"Ree-sult!" thought Becky, while Rachael made great play of checking her diary to make sure she was 'available'.

"I'll have to miss out," said a slightly crestfallen Sparks. "We're having a family meal at my gran's and she hasn't even got a telly!"

"Never mind, Sparks," chirped Ollie. "We'll video the game and I'll save you a large Marguerita and garlic bread."

"That's rich coming from you!" scoffed Becky, who knew that the chances of any food being left over when Sniffer Morris was around were virtually nil.

The High Street was a river of fluttering banners as the boys looked down from the top of Borough Hill. Soon, they had joined a procession of fans marching to the stadium with high hopes of a home win. The mood was friendly despite some of Dimaggio's steel-studded groupies who were trying to stir up trouble by throwing empty beer cans at Killerton supporters.

Suddenly, Max spotted a middle-aged man emerging from the betting shop. He was trying hard to be unobtrusive, but the combination of double-breasted yachting blazer and jogging bottoms had quite the opposite effect.

"Hello, sir!" he called, instantly recognising Charles Dudgeon, "Off to the match?"

"Not exactly," replied a startled and slightly embarrassed Head of I.C.T. "Mrs.Dudgeon and I quite enjoy the occasional flutter. Only a bit of fun, you understand. We decided to put a fiver on United winning today – but the odds aren't very good. With Lenny Dimmagio in the team we're favourites to win. We'd do much better backing Killerton, but I resisted that temptation. I wouldn't want to be disloyal to our lads, you know!"

"We'll make sure they don't let you down," laughed Ollie. "And you can give us our share of the winnings on Monday!"

Mr. Dudgeon smiled and hurried off into the supermarket.

Chants of 'Go! Go! Dimaggio!' were shaking the stadium as the boys clambered to their seats. Diana had put them half way back in the south stand, directly behind one of the goals. The atmosphere was electric and Ollie was ready with the camcorder when an ear-splitting roar brought both teams out onto the field.

"This is great footage!" he shouted, trying to stop his hands from shaking with excitement as he filmed Dimaggio warming up with his team-mates. "He's in amazing shape!"

As he zoomed closer, something struck him as odd. It was barely noticeable to the eye, but unmistakeable through the lens of a camera: the striker seemed preoccupied with someone or something directly behind their goal.

"Probably some stroppy Killerton fan giving him grief," Ollie muttered to himself, quickly dismissing it as the referee blew for the match to begin.

The home team was attacking their end of the pitch and the two boys had a spectacular head-on view of Dimaggio's speed and precision as he took on the Killerton defence; but Gostonborough's new line-up was slow to jell and, time after time, the team failed to press home its advantage. The first half ended with a score line of nil-nil and a trail of missed opportunities.

"We're playing like a lot of old women!" cried Ollie as the home crowd stirred with disappointment. "When are our forwards going to get it together and score? They could have had me up front for fifty quid a week!"

Although United looked more in control in the second half, the pressure from Killerton was unrelenting and, with ten minutes to go, the match was still deadlocked.Suddenly, the crowd went wild as a mistimed pass reached Dimaggio who powered the ball inches over the crossbar. Ollie zoomed in on the striker as he dropped back to face the goal kick noticing that, yet again, his attention was fixed on that same point behind the home goal. The mystery was starting to prey on his mind and, setting the camera aside, he looked down towards the front of the stand.

"Why aren't you filming, Sniff?" shouted Max, trying to make himself heard above the din. "Dimaggio's bound to put one away soon. Miss it and you're toast."

The words had scarcely passed his lips than Gostonborough came under attack again. Killerton's number seven was making a run for goal hotly pursued by Dimaggio who was using his speed to devastating effect in support of the defence. The crowd rose as he closed on his opponent, blocking him from centring the ball and winning possession five yards from the corner post. He tried to turn, but sent the ball spinning over the goal line.There were five minutes to go.The match was still drawn – and it was a corner to Killerton.

Ollie zoomed in on Dimaggio as he helped pack the goalmouth where his height could save United from last-minute defeat.

"Come on, Lenny! Clear it!" shouted Max, beside himself with excitement.

The players jostled for position as the ball arced

into the centre of the box and the striker made his leap. There was a mighty roar as the famous shaven head won the first touch, then a howl of dismay as, instead of flying to safety, the ball shot straight into the back of the net.

The sensational own goal sent Killerton's fans into a frenzy while the home supporters looked on in stunned disbelief. A demoralised Gostonborough eleven battled valiantly through the dying minutes, but it was too late to save the match. As the full-time whistle blew, Dimaggio stormed back to the dressing room, hurling abuse at the reporters and photographers massing at the tunnel mouth.

★★★

The atmosphere in the studio was subdued as the Newskids ate their pizzas and waited for "Match Of The Day" to start. Ollie hardly spoke. He sat alone with his camera,replaying Dimaggio's own goal over and over again.

"Come on, Sniff," said Max, handing him a slice of deep pan pepperoni with extra mushrooms. "No use crying over spilt milk."

"There's something weird about this," mused Ollie, ignoring the food and waving everyone over to watch his footage. "All afternoon, Dimaggio was looking at something in the crowd. He was doing it just before that corner was taken. Come and look."

Rachael raised her eyes to the ceiling.

"Can't you guys change the record?" she said. "It's a game, for gosh sakes, not open-heart surgery. So, the great Lenny Dimaggio goofed up. What's the big deal?"

"Just watch and you might find out," insisted Ollie, running the recording in slow motion and providing a running commentary as the striker's athletic frame rose into the air. "If you were trying to clear a corner, you'd keep an eye on where you wanted the ball to go, wouldn't you?" Rachael nodded. "But look at Dimaggio's eyes. They're fixed on his own goalmouth." She looked closer, suddenly seeing what he meant. "It's almost as if he *wants* it to go in...but why should he do that?"

"Perhaps "Match of the Day" will shed some light on it," said Becky. "Come on! It starts in two minutes – and don't forget we promised to record it for Sparks."

Max started the recorder and they settled back to watch the highlights. The TV cameras could film much closer than Ollie's camcorder and the striker's glances towards the south stand were unmistakeable. As the match wore on, they became more and more frequent until Killerton won the disastrous corner kick.

"This is like watching a scary movie knowing that a mad knife-man is about to tear someone apart!" said Becky who was roundly 'shushed' as the ball began its fateful journey into Gostonborough's net. Soon, the TV pundits were speculating on how a player of Dimaggio's calibre could have made such a gaffe. Did he miss his footing? Had he been pushed? Was it a momentary black-out? As the debate became more heated, the incident was replayed from every angle, ending with a slow motion shot from in front of the Gostonborough goal.

Suddenly, Ollie jumped to his feet and stopped the machine.

"Hang on, Sniff!" protested Becky. "The programme's not over yet. Sparks won't want to miss this!"

"I can't help it, Becky," he cried, hitting 'rewind'. "That slow motion shot could hold the key to all this. It's the only angle that shows the front of the stand where Max and I were sitting. Whatever was distracting Dimaggio may be somewhere in the picture."

The Newskids moved closer to the screen while he repeatedly re-ran the shot. They studied every detail around the goal as, again and again, Dimaggio headed the ball into the net. Finally, the image froze and Ollie pointed to a burly figure in a pale grey overcoat leaping to his feet in the second row of the stand. His hard-bitten features were contorted in a cry of delight and he was punching the air with a bejewelled leg-o'-mutton fist. It was the same man who, a few days earlier, had given Dimaggio a small fortune in fifty pound notes: the man known only as Smith.

"I think we might be opening an ugly can of worms here, Max," said Ollie. "Do you remember what Smith said to Lenny in the car park on Tuesday night?"

"I think so," replied Max. "He wanted to phone someone called Gold in the second half, didn't he? Do you think that's what put Lenny off his stroke – wondering whether he'd remember to make the call?"

"I don't think he *did* say 'I want to phone Gold in the second half,'" said Ollie mysteriously. "Remember, we were straining to hear that conversation through double glazed windows and there was a posse of

Premiership footballers shouting their heads off in the background. Suppose what he *actually* said was 'I want an *own goal* in the second half'? That would explain what happened this afternoon. Perhaps Smith was *paying* Dimaggio to throw the match – and was there in person to make sure he did what he'd been told."

Max looked dumbfounded as the pieces of the jigsaw started to fit.

"I think you might be right, Sniff!" he said. "And Dudgeon said that the bookmakers were giving better odds on Killerton to win. Jeez! If some sort of betting syndicate has got an England international in its pocket, there's no telling how much money it could make!"

Becky felt the hairs on the back of her neck start to rise as she sensed that they could be sailing into dangerous waters.

"We must be c..careful how we handle this," she said. "After all, it could just be some huge coincidence; but we'll soon have a chance to find out. We're interviewing the man himself next Tuesday – and I think Mr. Dimaggio may have some explaining to do..."

Chapter 12

BAITING A TRAP

The security man was his usual grumpy self when the Newskids arrived in force at Gostonborough United's training ground. Max had a plan – hardly an original one, in fact he'd borrowed it from William Shakespeare. It came from the scene they'd been studying for English Literature in which Hamlet hires a troupe of actors to recreate his father's murder, hoping their play will spook his wicked uncle into revealing himself as the killer.

Rachael and Becky were to interview Dimaggio together, lulling him into a sense of false security by posing as a pair of brainless bimbos who thought the off-side trap was a speed camera for motorists who drove on the wrong side of the road. Then, out of the blue, they would unleash two questions carefully designed to provoke a reaction that might reveal whether or not the foul-tempered striker was carrying a guilty secret. To make him feel at home, they wore pale make-up with black lipstick and rows of silver studs clipped to their ears and nostrils.

"Lenny's with the physio at the moment," said

Diana Sheldon, giving the girls a slightly old-fashioned look as she ushered them into the same room in which Ollie's blundering header had uncovered the stash of bank notes. "He's got to squeeze in a photo-shoot before training, so you'll have about ten minutes."

While she went to collect their interviewee, Sparks set up some small spotlights he'd borrowed from school and the girls took off their anoraks. Underneath, each of them was wearing a tee shirt with *'DIMAGGIO THE DESTROYER'* emblazoned across the chest.

"Don't be too disappointed if he doesn't fancy you," teased Ollie, busily setting up the camera. "But if Goston Dramatic Society needs a pair of ugly sisters for this year's panto, you're definitely in with a chance!"

Rachael was about to hit him when they heard footsteps entering the corridor and the sound of low voices.

"Nobody said I was being interviewed by a load of naffin' kids!" Dimaggio was grumbling.

"But I told you last Tuesday," protested Diana. "I even e-mailed your manager…"

"I never saw no e-mail," he snapped. "And I don't remember nothin' about no kids, neither."

"Not so loud, Lenny!" she hissed. "They'll hear you!"

The Newskids exchanged uncomfortable glances as the door handle turned. The prospect of meeting Lenny Dimaggio suddenly seemed much less appealing and everyone knew that, if the interview *did* touch a nerve, this could turn out to be a very unfriendly encounter indeed.

"This is Lenny," said Diana, looking far from relaxed as the striker pushed past her, completely ignoring Max's outstretched hand. "I'm sure you'll get along fine. Just ring me on the mobile if there's anything you need. I'll be in the office."

As the door closed, Dimaggio slumped into a chair and began to open his mail.

"I 'ope this ain't gonna take long," he grunted without bothering to look up. "Which one of you's askin' the questions?"

Although she was sharing the interview, Becky found the star quite intimidating and was already worrying about her stammer. Rachael sensed how uneasy she felt and did her best to distract him while Sparks adjusted the lights.

"Pleased to meet you, Len, I'm Rachael, but you can call me Raytche," she gushed, "My Guy Magazine has just voted you the sexiest man shorts. Does it feel cool when you read that sort of stuff about yourself?"

"Nah. It makes me feel a pillock," he grunted, turning to Becky. "Who are you?'

Becky took a deep breath but, before she could answer, Sparks gave the thumbs up that everything was ready.

"And *you'd* better not mess me about, neither!" barked the unco-operative star, suddenly rounding on Ollie. "You photographers get right up my nose with all your faffin' about."

Ollie smiled weakly, then took cover behind the camera as Max gave the signal for the interview to begin.

"What made you join Goston United, Len?" asked Rachael, fanning a whiff of cheap scent in the striker's direction.

Dimaggio shrugged and lifted his left foot lazily onto the desk top. She tried again.

"Have you always rated the club?"

"Not 'specially. Money's alright, though."

There was a long silence. Rachael decided that perhaps she wasn't his type and passed to Becky.

"Who are your b..best mates in the squad?" she asked, trying to control her nerves by slipping into character.

"Don't 'ave best mates. Can't trust 'em."

Becky gave him an encouraging smile, but it was no use. Dimaggio's eyes remained distant and cold. She wondered how a man who traded on being a role model and hero to millions of kids could possibly be so thoughtless and rude.

"How do you feel about playing at home for England in the World Cup?" she persevered.

This question seemed to raise slightly more interest, but before he could answer, a heavy metal guitar riff spilled from his kit bag and he began to rummage inside.

"Shut that naffin' camera off, will ya?" he shouted, glaring at Ollie as he took the call. "Yeah…'Allo, Smitty. Make it quick, will you?"

Everyone's ears pricked up at the mention of the name 'Smitty'. If Dimaggio was talking to the man called Smith, this conversation would be worth overhearing.

"No! Saturday's too soon," he mumbled, lowering

his voice and hurrying across the room. "Look, I can't talk now. I've gotta do an interview for a bunch of kids....No, I can't put 'em off. They're already in 'ere..."

The Newskids strained to hear more, but he was now leaning over the wash basin with his back towards them. Most of what he said was inaudible, but they did manage to catch a few words of the final exchange:

"...We'll do the business tonight. Get that fit little Irish secretary to book the usual table at One Eye... I'll be there at half eight."

Dimaggio ended the call without a 'goodbye' and Becky felt the anger rising inside her as he slouched back in his chair. This man was a rude, arrogant, self-important bully and she didn't trust him an inch. Stammer or no stammer, she was ready to wade in with her special question – and hoped it would make him squirm.

"Can we wrap this up, kids?" he whinged, flinging the phone back into his bag. "I ain't got all day."

"Maybe you can just settle a little score for us, Lenny," she said with an innocent grin. "Sharon Baker has been getting right up everybody's nose about the Killerton match last Saturday. She reckons you scored that own goal on p..purpose. What would you say to a soppy t..tart like that, eh...?"

Dimaggio's expression hardened and his right hand curled into a fist. If she'd been a man, Becky was sure he would have knocked her through the wall. But the fish was nibbling at the bait – and it was now up to Rachael to get it on the hook.

"Take no notice, Len!" she said. "Sharon's just a stupid slag. She was prattling on about some American geezer who made a fortune out of fixing horse races; but the cops sussed him when they found thousands of dollar bills hidden under his wardrobe. He got fifteen years, didn't he, Becky?"

There was no mistaking it. The word 'wardrobe' had acted like a trigger and the striker's eyes flashed towards the rickety cupboard standing exactly where Max and Ollie had replaced it; then something inside him seemed to snap and he lunged at the camera, covering the lens with a huge hand.

"I've 'ad enough of this!" he shouted, pushing the lights away and ripping the plugs out of the wall. "Get rid of all this rubbish and leave me alone. Go on! Get out of it!"

It was then that the Newskids knew for sure that Gostonborough United had a traitor in its ranks.

★★★

"He's as crooked as a dog's hind leg!" said Ollie as they parked their bikes outside Max's house and made their way down to the studio. "We've got to report him to the Club."

"And who do you think they'll believe?" asked Becky. "A multi-million-pound signing or a bunch of teenage kids?"

Ollie backed down, but everyone knew that Dimaggio would have to be stopped before he sent Gostonborough plunging to the bottom of the league.

"What wouldn't I give to be a fly on the wall

when he meets Smith tonight?" said Max. "If we could only film *that* conversation, we'd nail him once and for all."

"There are ways and means." Sparks piped up, his technical brain in top gear.

"Yeah! Right!" scoffed Ollie. "Lenny Dimaggio would be *delighted* if I burst in with a camera in the middle of his dinner. He'd probably kick my head in!"

"Hold on, Sniff!" said Max, sensing that Sparks had an idea. "Let's hear him out.What's on your mind, Sparks?"

"Well, it's possible to film people without them knowing you're there," he explained."If we could get into that restaurant before this evening's customers arrive, I might be able to bug Lenny's table and record every word they say."

"But how?" asked Becky. "This is Newskids on the Net, not MI5."

"I've got a little radio microphone in my kit," said the pint-sized boffin. "It's no bigger than a shirt button and works with a tiny transmitter the size of a five pence piece."

"Could it be linked up to my camera?" asked Ollie.

"No problem.The difficult bit would be hiding the camera."

Everyone thought hard.

"Maybe we could put it in a handbag on the next table." suggested Becky.

"But how would we get it there?" worried Rachael, who had serious doubts about the whole idea. "Even if we could afford a meal in an expensive restaurant,

Dimaggio knows what we look like. He'd have us thrown out before we even got to see the menu."

"Hang on a minute!" cried Max. "He might not want *us* around, but he wouldn't have a problem with my mum and dad..."

"No, Max!" Becky sternly interrupted him, "You can't set your poor father up again! He'll freak!"

"He'll be fine," he shrugged, completely carried away by the idea. "Anyway, it's their wedding anniversary next week. Mum's sure to love an early celebration."

"Some celebration!" said Rachael. "Wired for sound to a dangerous thug!"

Max wasn't listening. He was thinking back to Dimaggio's telephone call.

"He told Smith to ask his Irish secretary to book a table for eight thirty," he recalled. "Now what was the name of that restaurant?"

"It sounded something like 'One Eye,'" prompted Becky, who was already leafing through the restaurant section of Yellow Pages. "Let's see... 'Oeufs Cassés', 'O'Jay's Diner', 'The Orangery'..." Her finger travelled down every listing beginning with 'O',but there was nothing for 'One Eye' or anything faintly resembling it.

"We could have misheard," said Max, pacing the floor in frustration and chewing on a stem of his glasses. "Perhaps it's something that *sounds* like 'One Eye' – or maybe they call it 'One-Eye' for short. Let's think... 'One Eye'... 'One Eye'..."

"One eye smaller than the other?" giggled Rachael unhelpfully.

"One i-ota" tried Sparks, trying to keep a straight face.

"One Eye'm Sixty-Four…" said Ollie, giving up the ghost.

"Hold on a minute!" said Becky, who had widened her search into the night club section. "This could be what we're looking for. One Eyed Jacks. It's a casino in Penfold."

Max stood over her as she rang the number and continued to hover impatiently until the call was picked up.

"Hello. Is that One Eyed Jacks?' she asked. "G..good…Do you have a restaurant on the premises?...Thanks. I appreciate that." There was a pause. "They're putting me through to the dining room," she whispered to the others. "You're the actress, Rachael – how's your Irish accent?"

Completely unfazed, Rachael took over as a young Frenchman came on the line.

"Evenin', darling," she purred in a very convincing Dublin brogue. "This is Mr.Smith's secretary. I'd like to check a reservation, please."

"Un moment, mademoiselle, I will call Pierre."

There was a short wait, then the head waiter arrived.

"'Allo, Rose!" he cooed.

"Hi, Pierre. Mr. Smith has just asked me to check that his usual table is booked for half past eight. I can't afford any slip-ups – you know what he's like."

"But I reserve eet for you myself, ten meenits ago, don't you remember? Table fourteen, next to zee window. Don't worry. Eet will be ready."

"Thanks, Pierre. You're a diamond. Talk soon. Ciao!"

"Nice one, Rachael!" cried Becky, "Now it's my turn!"

Glancing quickly at the studio clock, she called the number again, anxiously biting her lip as she waited for an answer.

"One Eyed Jacks."

"Good evening. Would you put me through to Pierre in the restaurant, please?"

The Frenchman was annoyed at being disturbed again, but sounded as charming as ever as he took the call.

"Bonsoir. Pierre speaking."

"Hello there," said Becky, in her most sophisticated voice. "This is Sarah Montgomery, Personal Assistant to Nick T..Taylor of Brown, Macksey and Charles Advertising. Might you have a table for two at eight thirty? The one near the window next to number fourteen w..would be ideal."

"Un moment, s'il vous plait…"

Becky turned to the others, keeping her fingers tightly crossed that there *would* be a table for two next to number fourteen.

"…You are fortunate, mademoiselle," said Pierre, returning to the phone, "Table seven 'as just become available. What name deed you say?"

"T..Taylor,' said Becky. "Mr. and Mrs. Taylor. May I ask you just one more thing?"

"But of course."

"What time does the restaurant open tonight?"

"Service begins at seven thirty, mademoiselle. Merci et au revoir!"

It was now six o'clock. That gave Ollie and Sparks an hour and a half to cycle the five miles to One Eyed Jacks and wire Dimaggio's table for sound. It was the work of minutes to load the equipment into their saddlebags, then they were speeding towards Penfold. The others promised to follow once they had found a suitable handbag; but one big question mark still hung over the whole plan: what if Max's parents weren't in the mood for a romantic dinner for two…?

"Da-ad…" said Max, seeing the familiar look of alarm cross his father's face as he crept into the study. "What are you and mum doing tonight…?"

Chapter 13

ONE EYED JACKS

One Eyed Jacks was a sumptuous, if slightly glitzy, establishment boasting gold statues of the knaves of hearts, diamonds, spades and clubs above its porch. A red carpet, battened down with highly polished brass rods, hugged an imposing marble staircase that rose to a set of revolving doors through which the evening's well-heeled customers were starting to arrive.

The two boys had hidden their bikes behind the park railings on the opposite side of the road. It was a perfect base camp with plenty of trees and bushes providing cover from the casino entrance. While Sparks prepared his tools, Ollie kept watch on the burly security guard patrolling the porch.

"Get a move on, Sparks!" he called. "The restaurant opens in thirty minutes!"

"How are we going get past the gorilla at the front?" asked Sparks, cramming a small black box into the pocket of his anorak.

"Leave him to me!" replied Ollie who was carrying a clipboard and had placed a neat row of coloured pens in the top pocket of his blazer. "Let's go!"

They walked briskly across the road and climbed the staircase, but the security guard barred their way.

"No kids inside!" he growled.

Sparks turned on his heel, but Ollie scooped him back with the clipboard.

"Sorry to bother you, mister," he said with a disarming smile, "My mate and I have got to hand in our Geography project tomorrow and we're really up against it."

"Not my problem, son," interrupted the bouncer, buttoning a double-breasted dinner jacket across his massive chest. "They don't pay me to help kids with their homework. Now get lost!"

"Oh, do us a favour," persisted Ollie. "We're doing a survey on foods of the world served in our area's top ten restaurants. I'm sure Pierre wouldn't mind answering a few questions about your menu. It would only take a couple of minutes. Mum and dad are regulars here and they'll be really upset if you won't help us...I don't suppose your boss will be too happy, either."

Suddenly, the doorman changed his tune.

"I'll see what I can do," he grunted, pressing the transmit button of his walkie-talkie. "Front door to restaurant. Over!"

There was an electronic crackle, then a harassed French voice answered the call.

"Salle à manger. Pierre speaking."

"Hi, Pierre, it's Zack on the door. I've got two kids out here. They're doing some kind of project on foods of the world and want to talk to you for a couple of minutes."

The request drew a stream of Gallic expletives from the radio and Zack turned his back as he tried to appease the temperamental head waiter.

"I've already *tried* to get rid of 'em," they heard him mumble. "But the fat one says his mum and dad are regulars."

Ollie couldn't believe that he was hearing such a blatantly 'fattist' remark from a man five times his size but, discretion being the better part of valour, held his tongue as the unfriendly giant turned back.

"First floor, turn left at the painting of Mike Tyson and through the swing doors. Pierre's expecting you, but make it quick. The restaurant's busy tonight."

Pierre was clearly preoccupied when he met the boys at the dining room entrance. He was a short, fussy, self-important man wearing an immaculate dress suit and sporting a dapper black moustache.

"Bonsoir, mes amis," he said. "I will do my best to answer your questions, but I 'ave customers arriving soon. Depêchez-vous, s'il vous plait!"

Ollie and Sparks quickly took in their surroundings. It was a lofty, oak panelled room with a powder blue carpet and matching velvet curtains swagged back from three large, recessed windows. The question was which of these alcoves contained table fourteen? With Sparks pretending to take notes, Ollie launched the search with the first of a rather limited supply of questions on foods of the world.

"Erm...Do you have mussels on the menu?" he asked, leading Pierre across to the first window.

"Bien sur."

"Can you tell me they come from?"

"Chef buys zem from Penfold feesh market," replied the Frenchman, having to take very long strides to keep up. "Is eet absolutely necessary to walk about while we 'ave zees conversation?"

"It's very good for the digestion," lied Ollie, finding that the alcove housed table number ten.

As they moved on, Sparks saw that each table was decorated with a slim, porcelain vase containing a single flower. He knew that these would make perfect hiding places for the tiny bug. The question was how to plant it without Pierre noticing?

"Now cheese," continued Ollie, thinking on his feet. "I imagine you have an international selection?"

"But of course," scoffed their host, who was becoming more and more confused, "We 'ave Gauda from Holland, Brie de Meaux from France, some ripe Italian Dolcelate and goats chiss from zee foothills of the Pyrenees."

Sparks scribbled furiously until they reached the second alcove, only to be confronted by table two.

"Why do you need to know all zees seengs?" asked Pierre, following like a faithful Labrador.

"It's all to do with the Euro." bluffed Ollie arriving at the farthest window where, at last, they found table fourteen. Their hearts leapt as they saw that it was less than three metres from number seven, guaranteeing the hidden camera a perfect view; but pictures would be useless without sound and Ollie knew that it was now up to him to distract Pierre while Sparks rigged the microphone.

"Any chance of a quick tour of the kitchen while my colleague writes up his notes?"he asked.

"Out of zee question!" gasped the horrified head waiter. "Chef is *far* too beezee."

There was an uncomfortable silence. They were running out of time and Sparks knew that every second Pierre stood breathing down their necks moved the plan closer to disaster.

"Er...Can I use your toilet for a moment?" asked Ollie, edging across the room. "Then I'll ask my last question and we'll be out of here..."

As his friend disappeared into the gents, Sparks reached into his pocket, thumbing the tiny bug from its case and waiting for his chance to wire it into the vase. Meanwhile, Ollie had locked himself in a cubicle and was punching Max Taylor's number on his mobile.

"Hi, Sniff!" answered Max chirpily. "everything's set! Mum and dad are up for it and we're on our bikes!"

"Then you might as well turn them round and go home!" moaned Ollie. "The headwaiter won't let us out of his sight, so Sparks can't fit the bug. We need a diversion. You'll have to get Pierre to the phone and keep him talking. It's our only hope."

Pocketing the mobile, he flushed the loo and returned to the restaurant as calmly as he could. The Frenchman was standing immovably at table fourteen, arms folded, eyes locked suspiciously on Sparks.

"Well!" he snapped. "I am waiting!"

"Er...waiting for what?" asked Ollie, desperately playing for time.

"Your last question, of course!"

"Oh, that!" he laughed, wishing he'd never thought

of foods of the world and blurting out the first thing that came into his head. "Er...Do you have frogs legs?"

Just for a second, Sparks caught himself staring at the headwaiter's trousers. Then, thankfully, the phone rang.

"Attendez ici!" barked Pierre, sweeping back to the desk to take the call.

"You'll have to work fast, Sparks!" whispered Ollie once he was out of earshot. "That'll be Max. He's going to keep Napoleon talking, but we're on borrowed time."

While Ollie used his fuller figure to screen him from Pierre, Sparks set to work with the precision of a bomb disposal expert. First, he removed the single rose from its vase and laid it carefully on a napkin; then he went to work with a tiny screwdriver, listening constantly to the Frenchman who was getting more and more flustered as Max pretended to be a customer who had forgotten the name of the restaurant in which he was supposed to be dining that night.

"I am sorry, monsieur," he huffed, checking the reservations list for the third time. "I keep telling you, we 'ave no party booked in ze name of Wolstenholme ce soir."

"Then perhaps it's under Crozier," suggested Max. "Would you mind looking again...?"

Sparks knew that Pierre was reaching the end of his tether and his hands were trembling as he taped the transmitter into the neck of the vase and connected the tiny microphone; but before he could make it secure, the phone was slammed down and they were out of time.

"That's it, Sparks!" hissed Ollie, "Bury the mike or we're dead!"

Sparks replaced the rose and camouflaged the silver bug as best he could using the leaves at the top of the stem.

"You 'ave to go now," ordered the Frenchman, strutting towards them with an imperious wave of the hand. "What is zees question I've been kept waiting for?"

"Oh, that..." stalled Ollie, still hiding Sparks behind his ample frame while he cleared away the tools. "...Er...What's green and hairy and goes up and down?"

"Sacré Bleu! How do you expect me to know ze answer to a reediculous question like zat?" he blustered. "You tell me!"

"A gooseberry in a lift!"

It was a terrible joke, but flummoxed Pierre long enough for the boys to make a dash to the double doors.

"Thanks for everything, Pierre!" called Ollie. "I'll remember you to mum and dad. You're every bit as...er...French as they said you were. Au revoir!"

They raced down the stairs two at a time, sprinted through the lobby and out into the freezing night air, almost colliding with Zack the doorman who gave them a long, hard stare. Seconds later, they had reached the safer side of the park railings where Max and the others were waiting. Poor Sparks was soon under pressure again as four pairs of eyes watched him connect a small radio receiver to Ollie's camera. If he'd done his job well, tomorrow night's programme would rock English football to its foundations; if not, Lenny Dimaggio would be free to cheat again. Slowly, he pulled the headphones to his ears and gingerly turned up the volume; then his eyes sparkled as he heard Pierre barking instructions to his team of waiters. Table fourteen was wired for sound!

It was just after eight thirty when Nick Taylor's V.W. Beetle drew up outside the casino. Max had hoped to have his parents installed at their table long before Smith and Dimaggio arrived and was concerned that they had cut it so fine; but his blood froze when Zack moved to the driver's window and began a heated conversation with his father.

"Whatever's going on?" he murmured, "They'll be here at any moment. Is dad on a double yellow or something?"

After several nerve-racking minutes, Zack directed Mr. Taylor to the car park and swaggered back up the stairs, blowing into cupped hands as he disappeared into the warmth of the lobby.

"Quick, Sniff!" called Max. "We'd better give mum the camera before The Incredible Hulk comes back."

Mr. Taylor was locking the doors of the Beetle when the Newskids arrived breathlessly in the car park.

"What's up, dad?" asked Max.

"Our friend on the door won't let me in without a tie," said his father sheepishly. "Not a great start, eh?"

Max looked at his mother, whose silence spoke a thousand words; then he noticed how pretty she looked in her chic little red dress and felt really proud of her.

"Don't worry, dad," he said, taking off his school tie. "Wear this! If anyone asks, tell them you're a member of The Bridgemont Club!"

Mrs. Taylor had to smile as her husband put on the purple neckwear. It was far too small and clashed horribly with his brown, hounds tooth sports jacket – but at least it would get them into the restaurant.

"And here's an important fashion accessory for you, Mrs. T!" added Ollie, handing over a green handbag containing the camera. "There's a little hole for the lens cut out of one side. Just point it at table fourteen and frame Dimaggio and Smith using the handles like rifle sights; but whatever you do, don't forget to hit the record button!"

Mrs. Taylor was about to point out that a large green patent leather bag wasn't the perfect accessory to a red designer dress when a black Lexus glided into a space at the opposite end of the car park. Max and Ollie crouched out of sight as Smith emerged, zapped the lock and strode off towards the front entrance.

Studying his reflection in the V.W's wing mirror, Max's father gave the tie a final tweak and took his wife's arm. It was then that Max realised that he could be placing his parents in danger and remembered how much he loved and owed them.

"Good luck, mum and dad," he whispered. "You're on!"

Mr. Taylor swallowed hard and glanced at his wife.

"I suppose a McDonalds is out of the question?" he asked.

Chapter 14

DANGEROUS ENCOUNTERS

Max's mother clutched the handbag to her chest as Pierre swept grandly over to table seven offering menus and a wine list. The restaurant was almost full and the strains of Vivaldi's 'Four Seasons' played quietly in the background, creating a relaxed and convivial atmosphere.

"Bonsoir, madame et monsieur. Would you like to order aperitifs?"

"Two Kir Royales, please," requested Mr. Taylor, trying to sound calm, but conscious of the burly figure hunched at the next table.

"Certainement, monsieur."

Mrs. Taylor knew that Dimaggio could arrive at any moment and needed to position the camera. As the headwaiter summoned a minion, she glanced uneasily at Smith who was staring out of the window. Seizing her chance, she slid the handbag slowly towards the edge of the table and leaned forward until her head was level with its two handles;but as she closed one eye to home in on the target, she was horrified to see his craggy face glaring back.

"Oh, damn it!" she shrilled, springing back as if someone had given her an electric shock. "Contact lenses! Always popping out at the most awkward moments!"

Smith scowled and turned away without a word.

Back in the park, Max was a bundle of nerves as he listened through the headphones.

"Good on you, mum!" he murmured, relieved that his parents had weathered the first storm.

A distant church clock was chiming the hour as Becky took her turn to listen in.There was still no sign of Dimaggio and she could hear Smith cursing under his breath as the Taylors ordered their meal. Max was worrying that they might finish before the meeting even took place when, suddenly, the green Aston Martin roared into view and Gostonborough's new signing sprinted up the staircase, tossing the keys to Zack the doorman as he disappeared through the revolving doors.

Heads turned when Lenny Dimaggio entered the restaurant. He looked every inch the superstar in a black Versace suit and gold tie. Smith raised a hand as he made his way across the room – and Mrs. Taylor pressed the record button.

"What are they saying?" squeaked Ollie, beside himself with curiosity; but Becky put a finger to her lips. She didn't want to miss a second of the conversation at table fourteen.

"You'd be late for your own funeral!" Smith was grumbling.

"Give it a rest!" moaned Dimaggio. *"You know what they say about geese and golden eggs. If I were you, I'd shut my mouth before this one stops laying!"*

"Would you like to order aperitifs, Messieurs?" came Pierre's voice, politely interrupting them.

"Two lagers!" demanded the striker. *"And make it quick, mush."*

A clapping of hands indicated that Pierre was calling a waiter and, once the coast was clear, the two men began to talk.

"Where have you been, Len?" muttered Smith, *"I've been kicking my heels since half past eight."*

"Let's just say she's blond, five foot eight and leave it at that, shall we?"

"That's good enough for me, but your missus might not be so understanding."

"Don't come the preacher with me! What the eye don't see, the heart don't grieve over…"

"Pig!" snapped Becky with utter contempt; then she recoiled as the voices were drowned by a succession of heavy thumps and a burst of crackling interference.

"S..something's wrong!" she called, passing the headphones to Sparks who furrowed his brow.

"One of them's fiddling with the vase!" he cried. "There's nothing we can do except hope he finds something else to play with."

Fortunately, the waiter chose that moment to arrive with the drinks. There were two gentle thuds as beer glasses were placed on the table, then the banging stopped.

"Are you ready to order now, messieurs?" asked a young man's voice.

"Fillet steak and a Salade Niçoise for me." said Smith.

"And I'll 'ave the Chateaubriand with plenty of

mushrooms," added Dimaggio. *"And don't forget the brown sauce, do you hear?"*

"Très bien, Monsieur."

By now, Mr. and Mrs. Taylor had started their main course and were eating as slowly as possible to give table fourteen time to catch up. The camera rolled on as Smith handed back his menu and glanced furtively round the room. Becky pressed the headphones tightly to her ears, sensing that the moment had come for the crucial discussion to begin.

"Now here's the word. Last Saturday was a good little earner, but the syndicate thinks we can top it. So this is what I want you to do this weekend..."

Suddenly, a loud, watery plop stabbed her ear drums and the big man's voice was lost under more heavy static.

"We've lost the signal!" she panicked, flinging the headphones at Sparks who turned as white as a sheet as he heard a low-pitched rushing sound as though someone was drowning in a tub of water.

"I don't believe it!" he groaned.

"What's happening?" shouted Max, distraught that the plan was falling apart at its most crucial stage.

"I didn't have time to fix the microphone properly. All that banging must have dislodged it. It's fallen into the water at the bottom of the vase."

Max clenched his fists in frustration, but tried to stay calm. He decided that there was only one way to save the situation and quickly called his father's mobile number.

"Please let him have it switched on!" he breathed as he waited for the ring tone to start.

Mr. Taylor had just taken a mouthful of spinach when he felt the phone vibrate in his jacket pocket. Diners frowned their disapproval as he answered the call, covering his mouth with the lapel of his jacket in a rather pointless attempt to be unobtrusive.

"Listen carefully, dad," said Max, his heart pounding like an express train. "They've just started the conversation we need to record and the microphone has slipped into the bottom of the vase. You've got to replace it – and you must do it *now!*"

His father's appetite suddenly vanished and he turned quite pale.

"Are you alright, love?" asked Mrs. Taylor, seeing her husband staring at the rose on table fourteen as though he were in a trance; but Nick Taylor's creative mind was clear and alert. He knew that Smith and Dimaggio were unlikely to get rough in full view of the other diners and was focusing all his attention on the single bloom, imagining he was at work at the advertising agency, brainstorming ideas for a television commercial. Suddenly, the inspiration came and he strode over to Dimaggio's table, ruffling his hair and perching his reading glasses on the end of his nose.

"I must apologise for this interruption," he began, with the air of an absent-minded professor. "My name is Harvey Peat, Research Fellow in Botanic Studies at Birmingham University and Honorary Member of The Royal Horticultural Society."

If looks could kill, the expression on Smith's face would have put Mr. Taylor into intensive care; but the two men were so taken aback by his unexpected appearance that they let him continue.

"I have dedicated most of my professional life to the conservation of Hellusius Parventus, commonly known as the wrap-over rose," he explained. "It's on the verge of extinction and you have before of you one of the most magnificent specimens I have ever seen."

"Very interesting," shrugged Dimaggio. "Now get lost!"

But Mr. Taylor pressed on, undeterred.

"If you'll permit me to borrow the stem for a few minutes, I will make some sketches and trouble you no further."

Puzzled glances passed between the two men, but neither wanted to draw attention by causing a scene in the restaurant.

"'Urry up, then," growled Smith. "Take it and bog off!"

Mr. Taylor gently removed the porcelain vase and walked back to his place, cradling it like a new-born baby.

"Helucius Parventus, my dear!" he announced, placing the rose reverently in front of his wife who looked utterly bewildered as he continued his eulogy. "Look at those magnificent petals, light and delicate as gossamer itself!" With every word, he leaned further towards her until he was close enough to whisper: "The microphone's slipped! I'm going to the gents to replace it. You *must* keep them talking until I get back!"

Mrs. Taylor swallowed hard as her husband picked up the vase and hurried off to the cloakroom. She knew nothing about football and the prospect of making conversation with one of the world's leading strikers was utterly petrifying; she also knew that this mission was important, not only to Max but to the whole of Goston. That gave her the courage to approach table fourteen.

"He's...er... quite harmless," she faltered, fixing Dimaggio with her most charming smile. "He loves his flowers almost as much as you must love your football..."

The two men stared at her as she stumbled on.

"...Er...they're quite similar in many ways, aren't they...? Flowers and football..."

There was no response. "...I mean in the sense that people feel passionate about them...not in the sense that flowers can actually *play* football...that would be ridiculous...they haven't got legs for a start...they'd be hopeless in seven-a-sides."

She gave a girlish giggle, but Smith and Dimaggio remained stony-faced.

Meanwhile, Mr. Taylor was standing over the washbasin, straining the flower water through his fingers. The silver bug quickly dropped into his palm and he dried it under the hot air jet, almost deafening Sparks who was still listening through the headphones.

Back at table fourteen, Mrs. Taylor was struggling for clarification of the off-side rule, buying her husband vital extra seconds to wedge the microphone back into the neck of the vase with a piece of wet toilet tissue before dashing back to the restaurant.

"Ah! I see you're keeping everyone entertained, darling," he said, restoring the flower to its rightful position on table fourteen. "Sorry I took so long, but it was touch and go separating the stamen from the anthers."

Then, apologising once again for the intrusion, the Taylors returned to table seven.

"Nice going, dad!" said Max, almost cheering as sound was restored. "I don't know how you pulled that off, but you're a hero for doing it!"

It was now Ollie's turn for the headphones but, for several minutes, all he could hear was the clattering of knives and forks punctuated by gentle thuds as glasses were raised and lowered from the table.

"What's going on?" asked Max.

"Nothing," he replied. "Nobody's saying a word apart from your parents. They're just ordering second puddings to keep their table."

Suddenly, his body tensed as a voice came through – but it was the head waiter's.

"Was the Chateaubriand to your liking, monsieur?"

"Not bad, dad!" said Dimaggio. *"Now make yourself scarce, will you? We've got business to discuss."*

The whole team was clamouring to know what was happening, but Ollie raised an arm to quieten them.

"Shhhh!" he hissed. "This sounds more promising!"

There was a pause while plates were cleared, then Smith began to speak.

"The syndicate wants you to lose to Athletic on Saturday."

Ollie's eyes glinted and he gave the others an affirmative nod.

"No way!" retorted Dimaggio. *"I stuck my neck out*

far enough with that own goal – if I try something else on Saturday it'll be too naffin' obvious…"

"What's the matter, Len?' growled Smith, *"Bottling out on us, are you? What if I said there was an extra hundred grand in it? Would that ginger you up a bit?"*

"It ain't about the money. Tell 'em I'll throw the Debton match in three weeks time. Their central defender's an animal. I could let him nobble me all day and no-one would suspect a thing."

Five minutes later, the team had all the evidence it needed to blow the match-fixing scam out of the water. The following evening's Newskids on the Net was set to send shockwaves through English football – and put an end to Lenny Dimaggio's career.

"Let's not push our luck," said Max, grabbing his mobile. "It's time to get mum and dad out of there."

It was just after ten when Mr. and Mrs. Taylor emerged from the casino and joined the Newskids behind the park railings. They looked slightly shell-shocked, but were otherwise unharmed.

"I don't want to see another profiterole as long as I live!" said Mrs. Taylor, puffing out her cheeks to show how full she was.

"And from now on, roses are my *least* favourite flower!" added Mr. Taylor, pulling the tiny bugging device from his jacket pocket.

"How did you manage to rescue that?" asked Sparks in amazement.

"Let's just say that Pierre and I came to a small financial arrangement," he smiled. "I told him that a Hellusius Parventus would be the perfect souvenir of our anniversary dinner and he brought the vase over to our table. Smith and Dimaggio were so busy arguing that they didn't even notice. The French are a very romantic race, you know!"

Everyone laughed as Mrs. Taylor returned the handbag to Ollie and took her husband's arm.

"Thank goodness I'm not married to James Bond," she joked. "I don't think my nerves would stand it – and I don't want you spending any more time in that studio tonight, Max. There's been enough excitement for one day and it's school in the morning."

The Newskids thanked the Taylors who crossed the road to collect their car.

"Do you think your mum would mind if *I* called in at the studio, Max?" asked Ollie, waving as the V.W. turned onto the main road and sped away towards Goston. "I'd like to get this stuff edited before bed. We're live at seven tomorrow and I won't have time after school – there's that essay to write."

"O.K., Sniff." said Max. "But don't be all night, will you?'

"No way. I'm knackered. You guys go on ahead while I pack up the gear. I'll probably catch you up."

The others cycled off leaving him disconnecting the equipment and loading it into his saddlebag. There was no room for the green handbag, so he hung it over the handlebars and was just pedalling out of the park when a shout rang out.

"Oi! I want a word with you, son!"

His heart sank as he saw Zack the doorman signalling to him. Quickly dismounting,he wheeled his bike to the foot of the staircase, wondering if Pierre had landed them in trouble.

"You kids left a clipboard and a load of coloured pens here this afternoon," said the barrel-chested bouncer. "Do you want to take 'em now?"

"No worries," said a relieved Ollie. "We've kept all our notes. You can give the pens to your kids...if you've got any, that is..."

Zack glanced over his shoulder as he heard a group of customers leaving the casino. Ollie followed his gaze, then froze as he spotted Smith and Dimaggio emerging through the revolving doors.

"Goodnight, Mr. Dimaggio," said Zack, handing over the keys to the Aston Martin. "She's in the usual place."

Ollie gripped the handlebars tightly as the two men swept past him; then Dimaggio paused and slowly turned, his eyes narrowing as he remembered the interview in his dressing room that afternoon.

"What's up, Len?" asked Smith. "Did you forget something?"

"No. Everything's cool." said the striker, hanging back long enough for Ollie to know that he was suspicious; then, to his relief, he turned away.

As the two men walked on, Ollie wheeled his bike to the other side of the road and was about to mount up when Dimaggio stopped dead in his tracks and stared at the green handbag. The teenager knew that this was no time to hang around and cycled away for all he was worth, his stomach gripped by the same tingling sensation he remembered as a child when, on dark winter nights, he would run upstairs three at a time, imagining that ghosts were on his tail.

His lungs were almost bursting by the time he reached the little post office in Senton.

It was the half way point of his journey and, taking a cautious glance over his shoulder, he freewheeled into Bramble Hill Lane, a lonely short cut through thick woodland that was seldom used by motorists after dark. His aching legs quickly recovered and he was beginning to build up speed again when a pair of headlights swung into the lane behind him.

"There's nothing to worry about," he told himself. "The driver must be lost. Whoever it is will probably turn round at any second."

But the car didn't turn. Nor did it show any sign of overtaking. It kept pace with him, hovering like a predatory animal. Suddenly, he felt very scared and was wishing he'd stayed with the others when another pair of headlights appeared from the opposite direction. He knew that, somehow, he would have to force the oncoming car to stop and waited for it to come closer. Forty yards…thirty yards…twenty yards...then he swung his bike directly into the vehicle's path. The driver braked hard, sending the wheels bumping over a kerbstone and skidding to a halt on the overgrown verge.

"Hey! Watch where you're going, son!" shouted an elderly man in a cloth cap, winding down his window as the first car glided past. Ollie tried to identify its driver, but the blackened glass offered no clues and gave an eerie feeling that perhaps there was no-one inside at all; then it accelerated and swept into the distance. "Got a puncture, have you lad?" asked the old man.

"No, sir. I'm…er…lost," lied Ollie. "I'm on my way to Goston. Must have turned off the main road too early."

"You're not that far away, son," he said, sounding relieved that Ollie wasn't a young tearaway bent on stealing his car. "Turn left at the bottom of the lane, straight on at the mini-roundabout, first right and follow the signs. Are you sure you're alright, lad? You look as though you've seen a ghost!"

The lights were still on in the Taylor household when Ollie arrived. He could see Max talking to his parents through the sitting room window, but decided not to disturb them. Instead, he let himself through the back gate and wheeled his bike to the end of the garden. There was no moon and he needed a torch to unfasten the padlock on the studio door. It was freezing inside and, eager to sneak a look at the recording before uploading it onto the P.C., he hurriedly unzipped his camera case.

"I'm really looking forward to this!" he murmured, rubbing his hands in anticipation.

Suddenly, there was a faint scuffling outside the window. Ollie picked up the torch and shone it into the garden. There didn't seem to be anyone around, but he wanted to make sure and stepped cautiously outside. The night was silent and still. He played the torch beam over the frost-covered bushes and flowerbeds, but nothing stirred. Dropping on all-fours, he checked under the shed and, finding nothing more than a bundle of tools wrapped in an old tarpaulin, assumed there was a fox about and returned to watch the evening's work.

The pictures were superb. Mrs. Taylor had managed to get Smith and Dimaggio right in the middle of the frame and every word they spoke was crystal clear. Ollie was soon so engrossed in their conversation that he didn't hear the door open quietly behind him; or the tell-tale creak of a loose floorboard. Suddenly, he froze in terror as muscular fingers were clamped over his mouth and chin.

"You're coming with us!" barked a voice, "One sound and you're dead!"

Trying not to panic, the schoolboy quickly realised that, if he was going to be kidnapped, any chance of escape might depend on maintaining contact with the outside world. He struggled furiously, making it as difficult as possible for the man to unplug the camera. Fighting for breath as his head was pulled further and further back, he made a frantic fingertip search of the desk top until his hand closed on the video-phone.Nudging the charge plug out with his thumb, he slipped it quickly into his anorak pocket just as his nose was covered with a rag that smelt of antiseptic. Then he blacked out.

Chapter 15

SNAKE

It was almost midnight. Mr. Taylor had put the security chain on the front door and was just making his way up to bed when the phone rang. It was Ollie's father. Max woke with a start and dashed out of his room onto the landing.

"…He was editing something in the shed," his dad was saying. "Max promised us it wouldn't take long. The light went out nearly an hour ago. I thought he'd be home by now."

Max knew at once that something bad had happened and blamed himself for letting Ollie cycle back alone. Throwing on a dressing gown, he ran downstairs and jammed his feet into a pair of trainers. The untied laces flayed his ankles as he flew down the garden, dreading what he might find; but the shed was deserted and securely padlocked. His friend must have finished editing and headed home – but where was he now?

A low, rumbling sensation greeted Ollie as he drifted slowly back into consciousness. He was lying in pitch darkness, his entire body aching with cramp. He tried to stand up, but cracked his head on a low metal ceiling; he stretched out his arms, but they were constrained by narrow walls. Suddenly, the floor gave a lurch and he reached out to steady himself. His hand rested on a hard, circular object held down with straps. Close to tears, he probed its cold, metal centre; then his fingers worked outwards, exploring a ring of thick rubber etched with strange designs. He realised then that it was a spare wheel. He was trapped in the boot of a moving car.

Meanwhile, two uniformed police officers were comforting Ollie's parents who were beside themselves with worry.

"Has Oliver gone missing before?" asked Sergeant Grainger as his colleague, P.C.Oakley, made notes.

"No. Never." replied Mrs. Morris, her voice tremulous and tense. "He sometimes keeps strange hours, but always lets us know where he's going."

"Any particular reason for the strange hours?"

"He's a cameraman for a children's TV news station," interjected her husband,"It's called Newskids on the Net. If an important local story breaks, he tries to be there to cover it."

"And could that be what he's doing now?" enquired P.C. Oakley, looking up from his notebook, "Covering a story?"

"Not to our knowledge," replied Mr. Morris, squeezing his wife's hand. "He went to Penfold at six to film something with his friends, then stopped off at Max Taylor's house in Goss Street to edit the recording; but his father told us he left just after eleven.He should have been back ages ago."

Sergeant Grainger checked his watch.

"Does your son keep a diary, Mrs. Morris?"

"No, he tends to lose things like that. He uses the calendar on his P.C."

"Then I suggest we log in and check. Perhaps there's something he forgot to mention."

As his parents led the police officers upstairs, Ollie was focused and alert. He felt in his anorak pocket, relieved to find that the video-phone was still there. The screen saver gave a comforting glow as he pulled it out and noted the time: ten past midnight. He remembered the studio clock showing just after eleven when he was taken and the engine sound told him that the car was travelling at average speeds along suburban roads. That meant that they would have covered about forty miles, but which direction were they taking and what was the destination?

By quarter past midnight, two C.I.D. officers had arrived at the Taylors' house to interview Max.

"When did you last see Oliver?" asked Detective Inspector Ellis who was in charge of the investigation.

"Just after ten outside the One Eyed Jacks casino in Penfold. We left him sorting out his gear – then he was coming straight on here to edit the recording. The light in the shed was on when I went to bed, so he must have got back alright. Twenty minutes later the shed was in darkness."

"Did Mr. Dimaggio and his associate actually *see* Oliver at the casino?" asked the D.I. "Take your time, son. There's no hurry."

"I don't think so," replied Max. "We were hiding in a park across the road; but I suppose they might have spotted him after we'd gone."

"But if the alleged recording was made without their knowledge, how would these gentlemen have known that he posed any threat?"

That question was bothering Max, too.

"I don't know." he said quietly.

"Look, son," continued the Detective Inspector, "Lenny Dimaggio may be a bit of a bruiser, but I don't see him as the sort of bloke who goes around abducting teenage kids."

"But I think he had a *reason*," insisted Max, "We interviewed him for our TV station this afternoon and he got really wound up by some of the questions. I can show you the recording if you like..."

"We'll examine video evidence in the morning," said Ellis, turning to his Detective Sergeant. "The priority is to locate the boy. If this *is* an abduction, it must have occurred somewhere between here and Oliver Morris's home. Maintain the all-cars alert and check C.C.T.V. recorded within a two mile radius between 2215 and midnight thirty. If the lad hasn't been located by morning, we'll go door-to-door. There may be witnesses to a disturbance – and I'm interested in any information that could lead to the recovery of the bike."

While the officers went to work, Ollie was steadying himself against the spare wheel, keeping one ear pressed to the back of the boot compartment to listen in on the two voices locked in conversation inside the car.

"Watch your speed!" said one. "This is one night we *can't* afford to get pulled over by the cops."

"Why don't we finish him off now?" asked the other, "We've got the film, so Len's off the hook."

"He wants to find out how much the kids know," replied the first man, who had a curious hiss in his voice. "But if Old Bill or any 'ave-a-go merchants come sniffin' round, we're to take him out straight away. Have you got that?"

Max felt deeply troubled after the police had gone. There was something about the whole hideous scenario that didn't add up. Even if Dimaggio *had* suspected Ollie of secretly filming his conversation, why had he waited for him to edit the recording and lock up the shed before carrying out the abduction? The answer came to him in a blinding flash and, taking the stairs three at a time, he made another dash to the end of the garden. There were only a few yards left to run when he slipped on a frozen paving stone and fell headlong towards one of the brick footings that supported the shed. What he saw next sent a shiver down his spine: Ollie's bike had been forced underneath.

Ignoring the pain from a badly bruised shoulder, he let himself in and booted up the P.C. One click on *'NEWSKIDS FILMS'* confirmed his theory: the last story had been edited four days ago. That meant that Ollie had been kidnapped *before* he'd set to work and the door padlocked to avert suspicion. Feelings of panic and helplessness began to overwhelm him as he searched the studio for signs of a struggle or any clue as to where his friend might have gone. His heart sank as he found the camera case discarded in a waste paper basket. Then he noticed that the video-phone had disappeared. That gave him hope. If it had found its way into Ollie's pocket, there was a chance of getting him back.

Ollie's heart almost jumped into his mouth as the video-phone screamed and the words *'STUDIO CALLING'* flashed in the window display. A split second later, he had smothered it with his anorak and squeezed the 'off' switch; then he stared into the darkness, praying his abductors hadn't heard and hardly daring to breathe until he was sure that the car wasn't going to stop. Suddenly, a surge of power told him that they had moved onto a much faster stretch of road and, very cautiously, he turned the phone on again. The clock showed midnight thirty. Desperate for a fix on his position, he selected 'My Location'.

Loading...

Two minutes passed...

...Loading...

"Come on!" he hissed through clenched teeth.

Network error.

His heart sank.

Max was hanging his dressing gown on the bedroom door when the first text arrived. He dived across the room, sending the lamp flying as he grabbed his mobile from the bedside table.

Travelling in car boot. Destination unknown. No GPS. Have been on the road for an hour and fifteen. Average speed 40. Probably just joined motorway. Will try to phone. Do nothing till I do. They'll kill me if disturbed. O.

With Ollie sending clues to his position, Max ran down to the study where his father kept a set of road maps. Clearing aside the mugs of pens and pencils, he spread a copy of *Routefinder General* across the desk and, by the light of an angle-poise, studied every motorway that passed within a sixty mile radius of

Goston. He quickly deduced that the kidnappers had joined either the M14 at junction 5 (50 miles north) or the M15 at junction 2 (45 miles south). But which…?

The driver braked hard and Ollie was tossed around like a salad as the car juddered more slowly over a very bumpy road surface. A sound of drilling indicated road-works and he counted the minutes until the engine powered up again.

At twelve forty-two, another text reached Max's phone.

Road-works. Down to 20 MPH for 12 minutes. Back to cruising speed now. O.

Max thought for moment, then his eyes lighted on a piece of yellow plastic lying in his father's in-tray. It was an A.A. membership card. Grabbing the house phone, he dialled the twenty-four hour Emergency Breakdown Service.

"Hurry! Hurry!" he murmured, drumming his fingers on the desk top as he waited to get through.

"Good evening. You're through to the A.A. Can I help you?"

"I hope so," he said, breathing faster as he reeled off the membership number. "I need to find out if there are any road-works in either direction near junction 5 on the M14 or junction 2 on the M15. Please hurry. This is really important."

"Hold the line, please…"

As he waited for the answer, Max called Becky's mobile; but, struggling to keep the land line handset pressed to his other ear, he accidentally rang her house phone.

"What time of night do you call this, Max?"

murmured Mrs. Roberts, waking from a deep sleep and reaching blearily for the bedside lamp.

Instantly awake, Becky threw off her duvet and raced onto the landing. "Who is it, mum?" she asked, opening her mother's door and rubbing her eyes as the light flooded the room.

"It's Max. Goodness knows what he wants at this time of night. You'd better take it in the kitchen and…" Becky was already half way down the stairs and her mother had to shout the rest of the sentence. "…I want you back in bed in five minutes. You'll be fit for nothing at school tomorrow…!"

Heart pounding, Becky picked up the extension and waited for her mother to hang up. "It's Sniff, isn't it?" she whispered, knowing that something was terribly wrong.

"Dimaggio's got him in the boot of a car," said Max. "They're probably on a motorway. Not sure which yet. Ollie's G.P.S. isn't working, but he can send texts and I'm trying to track them."

"Is he hurt?"

"I don't think so – but he says his life's in danger and we're to do nothing till he calls us."

"And what if he can't call us?"

Max paused, then gave a deep sigh.

"I'm trying not to think about that. But whoever's taken him has done it for a reason and isn't likely to make a move on the motorway at seventy miles an hour. We've got to find out where he's being taken, Becky. I want Newskids to go live before school. If Ollie can send back enough information, someone out there might be able to piece it together and guide us to him."

Becky felt sick with worry, but her mind was ice-cool.

"Listen to me, Max," she said. "Our viewers w..won't be expecting to see us live till tonight. It'll be pointless putting out an S.O.S. if no-one's watching – but lots of kids visit the home page before school on Wednesdays to see what's coming up in the show. I think you should go to the studio right now and p..put up a message – something like: *Newskids needs your help. Stand by for emergency bulletin at 8 a.m.* Write it in red, green, pink and orange stripes or anything else that grabs attention. The more people who see the webcast, the better our chances of getting Sniff back."

"I'm on it!" said Max, "Will you ring Rachael and Sparks?"

"Leave them to me. We'll be at your place at seven..."

He cut her off as the A.A. man came back on the line.

"Sorry to keep you, sir. There are carriageway repairs between junctions 8 and 9 north of Turlingham on the M14 with lane closures expected for the next five days. I'd give it a wide berth if I were you. It'll be murder round there..."

The engine died and Ollie braced himself to face his captors. For a few seconds there was silence, then two doors slammed and he heard heavy footsteps clumping over tarmac. Frightened out of his wits, he slipped the video-phone down the back of his jeans, then the boot lid opened and twin torch beams blazed into his eyes. He raised a hand, squinting through outstretched fingers for any feature that might identify the two silhouettes that towered over him.

"Tie his hands, Snake!" said the man with the deeper voice.

The other lowered his torch and leaned closer, but his face was covered by a black balaclava with jagged holes surrounding dark, hollow eyes.

"I wouldn't struggle if I were you," he hissed, binding the teenager's wrists. "Not unless you want to be sent home in tiny bits."

As Snake's cruel hands tightened the knot, Ollie saw that both index fingers were encircled with elaborate tattoos of coiled pythons. Trying to ignore the pain of the bonds cutting into his skin, he held the video-phone tightly against the base of his spine while the thug rifled his pockets.

"Hold up!" he rasped, finding a mobile phone. "The sooner we get this off him the better."

"Oh! Please don't take that!" begged Ollie whose wrists had lost feeling and were turning quite blue. "What harm can it do?"

Snake gave a hollow laugh and tossed it to the ground, grinding it to splinters with his foot.

"No harm at all – now!"

The fourteen-year-old pretended to cry. His old mobile had no SIM card in any case and was a small price to pay for diverting attention from the Newskids video-phone.

"Stop your snivelling!" shouted the other man, slapping him across the back of the neck as he tied a blindfold in place. Ollie was sightless now, but his other senses were working more keenly than ever. He was processing every detail of this invisible place and building a picture of it in his mind's eye.

The two men pulled him to his feet and he was marched across what seemed to be a huge car park swept by a driving wind that carried an unusual smell that somehow reminded him of holidays abroad.

"Ninety-one, ninety-two, ninety-three..." He counted each step until they reached softer ground where sighing branches gave shelter from the icy breeze.

"Wait here!" ordered Snake, walking ahead.

Ollie stood perfectly still, alive to the sound of twigs snapping underfoot and a heavy iron gate groaning open on rusty hinges.

"Twenty-eight, twenty-nine..." Thirty yards along a muddy path, they entered a large, damp building that smelt of newly-sawn wood. His legs buckled as the men dragged him up a rickety staircase to a third floor room where, at last, the ropes and blindfold were untied. In the dismal glow of a single light bulb, Ollie saw strips of ageing wallpaper peeling back over bare floorboards. The windows were barred and their broken panes let in a freezing draught that set a forest of cobwebs dancing on the ceiling. There was no furniture, save a row of dilapidated cupboards from which Snake was hauling a filthy rolled-up mattress.

"You'd better get your head down," he rasped. "You're being shipped out of here at half past eight on the dot – and don't try putting no lights on. We don't want to send out invitations to the Old Bill."

"Don't think we won't be watching," warned the other man, "If we see so much as a glimmer, we'll be back like a shot – and you won't find us so friendly next time."

Ollie knew that these were no idle threats and sank to his knees as the men turned off the light and locked the door. He was in mortal fear of what would happen to him in the morning and didn't move a muscle until their clattering footsteps faded on the staircase and the iron gate clanged shut. Then he was alone, in darkness, in an unknown cell,in the middle of nowhere.

★★★

It was 2 a.m. Max had made the changes to the home page and was sitting up in bed studying the map book and clutching his mobile phone. Then the call came.

"This is bad, Max," said Ollie. "These guys are dangerous. I'm scared."

"How many of them are there?"

"Two."

"Do you know where you are?"

"I'm on the third floor of some run-down building. It could be a timber yard or saw mill, but they blindfolded me the moment we arrived so I can't be sure."

"Can you access maps now that you're out of the boot?"

"No. There's not enough signal. The phone keeps trying to load them, then everything freezes and I get an error message. Whatever this place is, it's way out in the middle of nowhere. Did you get my texts?

"Yes. Those road works are probably on the M14 just North of Turlingham – but I could only go by what you heard in the car boot – that's not exactly satellite navigation. Do you remember how long it took to get from there to where you are now?"

Ollie could feel his brain slowing from tiredness and cold, but tried to stay focused.

"We stuck with the motorway for another seventeen minutes," he recalled. "Then they turned off onto a very winding road – and, from the speed we were doing, I'd say the driver knew it pretty well."

Max lifted the bedside lamp onto the duvet to cast more light on the map book.

"If my calculations are right, that would have been junction eleven," he murmured. "But the winding road could be any one of a dozen country lanes. Did you see anything when they took you out of the car?"

"I didn't get a chance, but we were in some sort of car park. They dragged me across it for about a hundred yards, then we took a muddy path through a wood to the building I'm in now. There's an old iron gate at the front if that's any help…"

Max scanned the map, tracing every centimetre with the point of a pencil, but the area was miles from any town and the existence of a car park seemed fairly unlikely.

"I'm struggling, Sniff!" he sighed. "Did you pick up anything else? Sounds, tastes,smells…"

The journey was beginning to scramble in Ollie's head, but Max's question triggered one other thought.

"There *was* a smell," he said. "Only very faint…a bit like firelighters. It reminded me of that trip to Teneriffe with mum and dad last summer."

A wave of adrenaline surged through Max's body

and the pencil lead snapped as he circled something on the map.

"Could it have been aviation fuel?" he said. "Because if it was, your car park may be Tambleford Aerodrome. It's off an unmarked road twelve miles from junction eleven. Are you near a window?"

"Yes – unfortunately," shuddered Ollie, pulling the collar of his anorak up over his chin. "But it's pitch dark outside. I won't be able to see anything till daybreak."

"Now listen up," urged Max. "We're going to put out a special live bulletin at eight o'clock. I'm already advertising it on the home page. Rachael will talk to you on the video-phone and I want you to send back pictures of every landmark you can see: shops, rivers, churches..."

"For goodness sake be careful, Max," pleaded Ollie, remembering what his captors had said and sounding very frightened indeed. "I overhead them talking in the car. They've been told to kill me if anyone tries to interfere – and they're keeping watch."

Max was scared, too – but tried to keep his friend upbeat and calm while he thought the situation through.

"Try to stay calm, Sniff," he said. "The chances of Dimaggio's gorillas logging on to a children's news site at eight o'clock in the morning are practically nil. That gives you one big advantage: you're in touch with the outside world and they don't know it – yet!" There was no answer. "Sniff! Can you hear me…?"

For a moment, the signal broke up; then a muffled sob reassured him that his friend was still there and a plan began to form in his mind. It was clear that any intervention by parents or police could prove very risky until Ollie's precise location was known. The element of surprise was key to giving any rescue party the upper hand.

"Stay with me, Sniff!" he continued, "There's nothing we can do until we know exactly where you are. Even if this run-down building is nowhere near Tambleford Aerodrome, the chances are that one of our viewers will recognise it and give us a fix on your position. Once we have that, we'll smash these guys. They won't know what's hit them!"

Ollie didn't answer. His reserves of strength and courage were slipping away.

"Don't let them take me, Max," he whimpered. "These people mean business. They're coming back for me at eight thirty and I'm going to get hurt…I know it. You *must* get me out of here…!"

★★★

By three a.m., the temperature had dropped to minus five. Ollie was huddled under a single sheet, his arms aching from flailing at the rats that scurried inquisitively around their new room-mate. Exhausted, yet too cold to sleep, he was past caring whether his gaolers were watching for a light; he knew that, unless he found some blankets, he would freeze to death before they came back. Struggling to his feet, he groped blindly along the walls until he found a switch that gave him an electric shock in exchange for the miserly glow of the naked bulb. One by one, he rifled the cupboards, but found only a tangle of sacks jammed tightly onto a shelf. Chilled to the bone, he began to measure them against his legs and chest, tossing the small ones aside and checking the others for insects; but as the pile dwindled, he realised that the sacks had been placed there for a reason: they were hiding a stack of small, transparent plastic bags. Gingerly, he pulled one into the light and squeezed the white powder that was packed tightly inside. Then a deeper chill gripped him. He had seen enough gangster movies to know that this was a drugs cache and he had stumbled across a fortune in heroin and cocaine. He was petrified now and prepared for a long, sleepless night.

Chapter 16

RACE AGAINST TIME

It was seven fifteen and the situation was as clear as it was terrifying: if the Newskids failed to secure Ollie's release by eight thirty, they might never see him again.

"How long to go?" asked Rachael, fiddling with the plug on a set of heated rollers."I didn't have a chance to wash my hair."

"Wear a hat if you're that b..bothered!" snapped Becky, whose nerves were at breaking point. "We're here to rescue Ollie, not win beauty contests."

Rachael instantly regretted her remark. She hadn't meant to sound callous. It was just her way of coping with the pressure.

"You're right, Becky," she said contritely. "I guess that was a pretty mindless thing to say."

"We won't get anywhere by fighting each other," warned Max, trying to keep everybody calm, "Lenny Dimaggio is the enemy; but remember: we still have no proof that he had anything to do with Ollie's kidnapping. Until we do, no-one is to start making accusations or we could find ourselves in big trouble. Is everyone O.K. with that?"

The rehearsal was tense with none of the usual banter. Rachael was to present the programme in front of a diagram Max and Becky had drawn with felt-tip pens. The route from the M14 to Tambleford Aerodrome was marked in blue and, using drawings and a red dotted line, they had depicted Ollie's journey across the airfield, along the woodland path and through the iron gate.

While Sparks made his final technical checks, Rachael paced the floor, repeating the facts to herself over and over again until every last detail was locked in her memory.

"Thirty seconds to webcast!" called Becky, glancing at the studio clock.

"I've got Sniff on the video-phone!" said Sparks, "It's a terrible signal. I hope it'll last out." Everyone turned to the grainy image flickering on the monitor screen.It was hard to believe that the person in the picture was Ollie. He was hunched in front of a barred window, his face deathly pale, eyes set in a fearful stare.

"T..ten seconds..." stammered Becky, choking back the emotion. "Three, two, one – cue Rachael!"

The young presenter breathed deeply, then turned to face the camera.

"Good morning and thank you for joining us for a special edition of Newskids onthe Net," she began. "This webcast is urgent. It may be a matter of life and death.At eleven fifteen last night, our friend Ollie Morris was taken from this studio by force. He's being held on the third floor of an unknown building that may be close to Tambleford Aerodrome off the M14. We're appealing to *all* Newskids viewers to contact us immediately if they know exactly where or what this building is."

With great precision, Rachael described the kidnappers' route, then Ollie's face appeared on the screen, the picture slightly unsteady as his hand trembled from cold and lack of sleep.

"Hi, Ollie!' she greeted him. "You're live to Newskids viewers across the country. What can you tell us about this place?"

Ollie lowered the video-phone for a moment then, finding the strength to hold it out at arm's length, spoke into its tiny lens.

"It's a run-down building that smells of damp wood," he croaked. "It could be a saw mill or timber merchants…maybe even a builder's yard…I can't say any more because they blindfolded me…" Suddenly, his voice trailed off as he thought about the two men who were probably already on their way to collect him. "Please help me!' he begged. "If I'm not out of here by eight thirty, I'm dead meat..."

Rachael almost wept as she saw the haunted look in his eyes.

"We need to see exactly where this building is, Sniff," she said, speaking slowly and clearly to keep him focused. "Can you point the phone outside?"

Slowly, the little camera moved towards the window, passing eerily between two metal bars and floating outwards through a broken pane. They saw a vista of trees with the distant motorway cutting through open fields beyond; otherwise it was an unremarkable country landscape.

Becky kept her eyes locked on the P.C., praying

that the information they so desperately needed would come through.

"That view could be anywhere!" whispered Max, knowing that every wasted second placed their friend in greater danger. "Ask him what else he can see, Rachael! We've only got fifteen minutes left!"

"We need more detail, Ollie!" said Rachael more urgently. "Can you move the camera left or right?"

There was a moment's pause, then the picture shifted again, taking in the edge of an airfield where a red helicopter was standing outside its hangar, rotor blades glinting in the early morning sunlight.

"Tell him to hold that shot!" hissed Max. "We *must* give people time to take it in and…"

He gave a gasp of dismay as Ollie's strength gave out and the image vanished from the screen. Rachael shot a frantic glance at Becky who looked up from the P.C., shaking her head.

"Come on, Ollie!" urged the presenter, "You must stay strong! Let's not give in to these guys! What else is out there?"

With a huge effort, Ollie raised his arm, but the camera's view was blocked by a branch directly outside the window. He turned his wrist to the left and the picture travelled towards a small clearing, then swerved across a cluster of elms.

"I think there was something in those trees!" cried Max, leaping to his feet, "Tell him to go back to them! He must be quick, Rachael! We're almost out of time!"

"Sniff! Can you hear me?" she called, trying to keep their friend alert. The camera moved up and down, as though it were nodding to her. "There may be something in those trees! Go back to them! And do it fast!"

The picture started to break up as the camera zoomed towards the thicket revealing a faded hoarding nailed to a broken fence. The lettering was difficult to read, but they could faintly distinguish the two words *HOT* and *PAINT.*

Suddenly, Becky sat bolt upright as, at long last, a single message arrived. The others were beside her in a flash, willing it to be the crucial breakthrough.

That's Hotshots Paintball Park. My dad built it in the woods behind Balderton's Saw Mill. I'm working on a plan. Tell Ollie to listen for my instructions. Imperative he does everything I say. Good luck. Andy Patterson.

★★★

The gate clanged and Ollie returned the video-phone to its hiding place in the back of his jeans. Andy's message had lifted his spirits and he scrambled under the blanket as footsteps mounted the stairs and a key rattled in the lock. With eyes half-closed, he peeped towards the door – hoping to catch a glimpse of his kidnappers' faces; but the masks were still in place and they seemed more threatening than before.

"Rise and shine, fatso!" called Snake, kicking him on the thigh as his accomplice unzipped a black holdall. Pretending to be waking from a deep sleep, Ollie managed to keep his wrists slightly apart as they retied the rope; then he was blindfolded again. He heard the cupboard door swing open and a succession of gentle thuds as the packages were tossed into the bag; then came a louder, more powerful sound that made him start in alarm: a helicopter was starting up on the airfield.

"Time to go!" ordered Snake, dragging him onto the landing. The chattering rotors grew louder as Ollie was manhandled down the three flights of stairs and pushed through the long room that smelt of sawn wood. Everything seemed to be happening at once and he was desperately listening out for Andy's instructions when a heavy plank caught his shoulder, jarring him sideways and breaking Snake's grip. At that moment, a single,clipped command cut through the din.

"Ollie! Get down!"

It was a voice you didn't question and Ollie dropped to the floor, wincing as a volley of gunshots sent the two men diving for cover. In the confusion, he slipped his wrists from the knotted rope and began tearing at the blindfold; but before he could untie it,Snake yanked him behind a pile of timber where his partner lay groaning on the floor.

"Cease fire!" shouted the voice.

The gunshots stopped and Snake peered cautiously over the planks, his dark eyes scanning the room like heat-seeking missiles.

"Who are you?" he shouted, seeing no trace of the mystery gunman.

"Show yourself and I'll tell you!"

As the big man climbed to his feet, Ollie pulled off the blindfold and blinked towards shafts of wintry sunlight that were streaming through the broken roof panels of a dilapidated warehouse filled with racks of timber.

"What do you want?" called Snake, searching for an escape route as an ugly red stain spread over his partner's body-warmer.

Suddenly, a tall, skinny youth wearing combat fatigues and a brown beanie hat appeared on top of a pile of pallets. It was Andy Patterson and he was cradling an automatic weapon.

"We want Ollie Morris!" he demanded. "Don't we, lads?"

"That's right!" echoed two similarly armed fifteen-year-olds in grungey trousers and Doc Martens emerging from behind a fork-lift truck.

"And we want him now!" added four more tough-looking customers walking out onto a gantry overhead. A look of alarm flickered across Snake's face as all seven gunmen aimed squarely at his midriff.

"You don't know what you're getting yourselves into!" he yelled. "If we're not on that chopper in thirty seconds, they'll come looking for us. You're not the only ones with shooters, you know. There'll be a bloodbath in here – and you'll be doing the filling!"

But Andy was in no mood for idle threats.

"Open fire!" he commanded.

Another barrage smacked into the wood-pile and Snake crashed to the floor. Ollie winced and put his fingers in his ears until the bombardment stopped; then he turned – preparing himself for the gruesome sight that lay at his side. But there was no blood; instead, both men were spattered with blotches of red, yellow and purple paint. Andy Patterson had rallied a hit squad of marksmen from the Hotshots Paintball Club – but the battle was far from won.

"Run!" shouted Andy, trying to get Ollie clear before the two men could collect their thoughts – but Snake was too quick for him. The paint balls had stung, but he now knew that the boys posed no real threat. As Ollie made his move, he grabbed him round the neck and pressed a razor-sharp blade to his throat.

"Drop the guns or I'll stick him!" he snarled, dragging his hostage into the open where the paint-ballers could clearly see the six inch hunting knife. "Now listen up! We're going out to the airfield now and I want you little scumbags to walk in front of us –and keep those hands where I can see 'em."

One by one, the dispirited paint-ballers dropped their weapons and shuffled outside, facing the advancing knife-man who kept an ever-tightening grip on Ollie's chest while his partner followed with the holdall.

"That's more like it!" hissed Snake. "Now, I want one of you to open the gate and we'll take the path through the copse. Keep your distance, mind!"

Andy heaved the gate open and the group backed slowly down a muddy tree-lined path until the helicopter came into view. Snake knew that he was home and dry and relaxed his grip on Ollie to sheath the knife; but that momentary lapse was exactly what Andy had been waiting for.

"Go, Ollie! Run for your life!" he yelled.

Before Snake could react, the air was filled with sharp reports and hundreds more paint balls flew from behind every bush, tree and hedge where the Junior

Hotshots had been waiting for their moment to open fire. Ollie dived for cover as the two men tried to ward off the hailstorm of missiles splattering their sticky contents over every part of their bodies; then, remembering his duty to Newskids on the Net, he pulled out the video-phone and quickly called the studio.

Max's stomach was in knots as he took the call. The special bulletin was coming to an end and everyone had begun to give up hope.

"Sniff! Are you O.K?"

"Yeah! I'm alright, Max! But the guys who kidnapped me are having a rough time. I can offer you some great pictures, but you'll have to be quick!"

Max turned to the others, almost crying with relief.

"Ollie's safe!" he shouted. "He says he's got some pictures for us. Hand over to him, Rachael!"

The team howled with delight as Ollie aimed the camera at the hullabaloo in the woods, ending the programme with a sequence to rival any Hollywood action movie.

"Get a move on!" the pilot was yelling as Snake and his accomplice raced onto the tarmac, arms flailing about their heads as if they were fending off a huge swarm of bees. "We can't take on fifty screaming kids!"

Suddenly, the helicopter began to lurch into the air and Newskids viewers were treated to spectacular coverage of Ollie's kidnappers clinging to the skids for dear life as it reared skywards with multicoloured bombs exploding over its sides and windows.

"How does it feel to be free, Sniff?" asked a jubilant Rachael as the chopper vanished over the horizon. Ollie panned the video-phone out of the sky and turned it on himself. The picture said it all. He and Andy Patterson were surrounded by the cheering Hotshots rescue squad – guns brandished triumphantly in the air!

"You don't know how good!" he said. "There's only one thing better – and that's the bacon sandwich I'm going to eat when I've had at least twelve hours' sleep! This is Ollie Morris for Newskids on the Net signing off from Tambleford Aerodrome!"

Chapter 17

THE ROAD TO WEMBLEY

The celebrations were short-lived. Lenny Dimaggio strenuously denied the children's allegations, and they had no evidence to prove that he was anything worse than an ill-mannered lout whose dazzling performances in a football shirt excused his behaviour off the field. Nevertheless, the Newskids now posed a real threat to some very dangerous people and, from the day Ollie came home, their lives began to change. They were constantly looking over their shoulders, always travelled in pairs – and no-one ever visited the studio alone.

Becky began to collect Dimaggio's press cuttings, hoping to find some snippet of information that might give credence to their story; but the usual stories of drinking, womanising and violent behaviour quickly disappeared. In their place came reports of a new Lenny Dimaggio: a man who took part in charity fun runs, opened centres for children with special needs and campaigned for a safer environment for the elderly.

"Who writes all this stuff?" asked Ollie in disgust as

he read the headline *'SAINT LEN'* in The Gazette. "He must have a great P.R. team, that's all I can say. They'll have him standing in for Father Christmas next!"

The striker's performance on the field changed, too. There were no more suspicious match results and he had soon notched up his twentieth goal of the season, earning Gostonborough United a place in the quarterfinals of the F.A. Cup. and winning over the hearts and minds of the community.

As winter turned to spring, Becky began to worry about Max. Ollie's kidnapping had affected him badly and the pressures of school work combined with the strain of running a television station were making him more and more withdrawn; but, worst of all, Lenny Dimaggio had become an obsession: it was as though he were putting his own life on hold until they could prove their story to the police and football authorities.

One April evening, she found an excuse to make some changes to the website and asked him to go with her to the studio. Max had always been reluctant to show his deeper feelings but, on this occasion, Becky's instinct had been right: he needed to talk.

"It's all my fault," he sighed, burying his head in his hands. "If I'd stayed with Ollie that night, Dimaggio would have been put away by now. We've let our viewers down, failed the fans – and I go cold thinking about the lives those drugs are wrecking now that they're out there on the streets."

"You can't keep beating yourself up, Max," she said, putting a comforting arm round his shoulders. "You didn't force Ollie to go back to the studio. O.K., we lost the evidence – but we'll get our chance to nail Dimaggio. It may not be this week, maybe not next month – but it'll come. Just you wait and see."

He laid his head against her shoulder and Becky felt happy as she stroked his hair, rocking him gently and soothing the demons away. She liked being strong for him and there was a closeness between them that she had never felt before. Slowly, she moved her face towards his and was about to speak when the door burst open and Rachael stormed in, oblivious of the special moment she had completely destroyed.

"Have you seen the new issue of *At Home With The Stars*?" she fumed, tossing a magazine onto the desk. "That creep has got some nerve. Their readers must be morons if they swallow this stuff!"

Max and Becky could hardly believe their eyes when they turned to the centre pages. The story was headlined *'AN IDEAL HUSBAND'*. It was packed with glamorous photographs of Lenny Dimaggio in his luxury home, grinning at the camera with his beautiful wife Terri, twin boys Luke and Dean and a pair of cute Labrador pups called Lily and Tim.

"Doesn't that make you want to throw up?" huffed Rachael. "We've got to do something, Max. The guy's a dangerous crook!"

A tide of anger surged through Max as he read the article. What right had this man to promote himself as a perfect husband and father when he had tried to have Ollie killed? There was only one way to hit back and, in less than an hour, a new panel had appeared on the Newskids site:

SHOULD WE ***REALLY*** *BE PROUD OF LENNY DIMAGGIO?*

At Home with the Stars says……Lenny is a devoted husband and father.

Newskids on the Net says………He's a serial womaniser who prefers clubbing and gambling to family evenings at home.

At Home with the Stars says……Lenny likes nothing better than a strawberry milkshake with the kids.

Newskids on the Net says………He has two convictions for drink-driving and has been barred from three local bars for violent behaviour.

At Home with the Stars says……Lenny will never refuse an autograph.

Newskids on the Net says………His manager smashed a young fan's mobile phone when he asked him to sign.

Although Becky had her misgivings, Max seemed brighter for having written the piece, so she decided to keep quiet; but it wasn't until they arrived at school next day that she realised the idea had been a terrible mistake. They were cold-shouldered by almost everyone they met and Max was completely baffled until John Atwood, the school football captain, pulled him into the visitors' changing room and gave him a piece of his mind.

"Who do you think you are, Taylor?" he shouted. "Dimaggio walking out in the middle of one of your poxy TV interviews doesn't give you the right to slag him off. Everyone knows he can be a bad boy, but that man has done wonders for Gostonborough this season; he's made us proud to live here and we'll be prouder still if he scores a few for England in the World Cup. You're well out of order here, Max, and if you and your bunch of hacks say another word against him, you won't have any viewers *left* at this school."

To drive his point home, he shoved him backwards into a tangle of nets and stormed out. Max lay in silence, feeling crushed and alone. Newskids on the Net was powerless to fight Dimaggio's ruthless P.R. machine. The striker had won. He was in bed before ten that night, wanting to cut himself off from the world. Everything seemed so unjust and his dreams of a life in journalism were beginning to fade.

★★★

"There's something for you from the BBC!" called Mrs. Taylor, collecting the post next morning. At first, Max was in no hurry to get out of bed, then curiosity got the better of him and he shuffled downstairs to the kitchen. His mother was concerned that he'd been feeling so low, but some of the old spark returned when he opened the letter.

"You'll never believe it, mum!" he gasped. "We've won an award!"

It was a much needed shot in the arm and he began to read aloud:

"In recognition of their outstanding achievement in tracing missing schoolgirl Josie Steed, we are pleased to invite NEWSKIDS ON THE NET to receive Junior Community Action Awards in a special programme live from BBC MediaCity UK at 6.30p.m. on Saturday, April 23rd.

In addition to Helping Hand statuettes, all winners will receive special prizes presented by our host, Greg Armstrong of BBC News."

The next few weeks were not the happiest of times for the Newskids. Despite their good fortune, they continued to suffer some hostility at school, but managed put it all behind them when they arrived at BBC MediaCity in Salford on the big day. Preparing to face the cameras, Max was thrilled to see the expressions of delight on the others' faces when Greg Armstrong himself paid them a visit in the make-up room.

"Hi, gang!" smiled the newsreader. "I had a feeling we'd meet again one of these days – but I wasn't expecting it to happen quite so soon! I'm not allowed to tell you about your prize until we're on the air – but I think you're going to like it! See you in the studio. Good luck!"

It was the proudest moment of their lives when, live to a TV audience of millions, Newskids on the Net were called to receive their statuettes.

"I've had the privilege of meeting these youngsters before," said Greg as the applause died away. "They started their own internet news service four months ago and were responsible for finding the missing school girl, Josie Steed. In recognition of their initiative and achievement, Max, Becky, Ollie, Rachael and Akbar are to be guests of BBC Sport at a semifinal of this year's World Cup at Wembley Stadium." The Newskids were over the moon, but there was more to come: "The two-day trip will include a tour of the stadium, a chance to meet the teams – and a night in a luxury hotel."

The studio audience erupted; Rachael and Becky hugged each other in delight; Ollie and Sparks shook hands with Greg and Max drank in the applause. His dreams for the future were burning brightly again.

★★★

School life became more tolerable after the programme and, although some children still begrudged them their trip to Wembley, something more important was soon occupying everyone's thoughts. On June 10th, England opened its doors to the cream of world footballing talent and pupils and staff joined families across the globe watching the World Cup opening ceremony on TV. It was a breathtaking spectacle. Fireworks glittered over Wembley Stadium whose massive arch crowned an arena in which thousands of dancers and gymnasts were weaving miles of coloured silks into the flags of every competing nation.

"I wonder who we'll be watching in the semis?" mused Ollie, putting his feet up on the news desk as Mexico and Senegal lined up for the opening match. Max had been asking himself that question since the day of the awards programme, but was now grappling with another problem: if one of the teams turned out to be England, how would Lenny Dimaggio react when they met him after the game?

For the next five weeks, the nation was gripped in a frenzy of football. Thousands of fans took time off to watch the drama unfold, others were taking televisions and radios to work while school children up and down the country were allowed free periods to follow the England campaign. Lenny Dimaggio seemed invincible. His shaven head and liking for body studs earned him the nickname 'Silver Bullet' as he powered home goal after goal, finally toppling Nigeria with a driving header in the seventieth minute of the quarterfinal. England were through!

★★★

It was a sun-drenched Wednesday morning in mid-July when a white stretch limousine hummed into Goss Street. This moment was almost beyond Max's wildest dreams. They were on their way to Wembley! In just over twenty-four hours, England's top players would be lining up against Germany in a World Cup semifinal – and Newskids on the Net would be right at the heart of the action.

National flags flew proudly from tall white poles lining the driveway to the Grand Hotel where the limo glided to a halt and John, their chauffeur, slid back the privacy window.

"Not bad for a B&B!" he joked as a commissionaire, resplendent top hat and white gloves, opened the door. "I'll wait here while you check in. You've got a tour of the stadium this afternoon, then it's back to the hotel for dinner and a good night's rest. Kick-off's tomorrow at three."

A posse of photographers surrounded them as they stepped out of the air conditioned stretch into the intense summer heat. Rachael was in her element as the cameras followed them into a lobby teeming with

V.I.Ps and reverberating to a hubbub of conversation in a dozen different languages.

"Do you have a reservation, miss?" asked a girl at the reception desk.

"Yes, I d...do," said Becky, feeling slightly overwhelmed as she set her case down on the marble floor. "My name is Rebecca Roberts. I'm with Newskids on the Net. We're..."

Before she could finish, pandemonium broke out by the front door where the paparazzi had spotted a group of glamorous, deeply tanned women in designer jeans and micro-miniskirts wheeling Louis Vuitton suitcases. Knowing that wives and girlfriends of the England squad always guaranteed lucrative picture spreads, the photographers closed in, shouting at the tops of their voices and elbowing each other out of the way to get the best shots. The women seemed to take it all in their stride and Becky heard them laughing and chattering as they stood behind her in the queue.

"Thank you, Miss Roberts," smiled the receptionist, handing her a key. "We've put Newskids on the Net in adjacent rooms. Yours is 417. Take the lift to the fourth floor and turn right. Enjoy your stay."

The bedrooms were an adventure in themselves, but there was no time to try out the en suite jacuzzis, widescreen surround-sound TVs – or sample the goodies in the mini-bars. Dumping their bags, they dashed straight back to the limo which was soon cruising towards the stadium, treating them to their first close-up view of the Wembley arch. It looked even bigger in real life than it had on television: a massive steel frame soaring like a giant rainbow a hundred and thirty metres into the London skyline.

Rows of BBC television and radio trucks were parked nose to tail, forming a media village on basement level one. As the stretch glided to a halt, a young, sandy-haired producer wearing a smart open-necked shirt emerged from one of the trailers. He had a walkie-talkie strapped to his belt and carried a bundle of schedules.

"You must be Newskids on the Net!" he exclaimed, tucking the documents under one arm and shaking their hands. "I'm Paul Cooper. I'll be your contact for the next day and a half. I thought we'd start with a tour of the stadium. Are you guys up for that?"

"You bet!" cried Max. "Do you mind if we interview you along the way? We've brought a video camera so that we can share this trip with our viewers in next week's show."

"No problem," said Paul. "I'll just drop these running orders into the sound truck and we'll be on our way."

Ollie's heart raced when they reached the entrance to the players' tunnel. As he stood filming the towering stands, he was trying to imagine how it would feel being a member of the England squad, waiting to walk out and play for the glory of your country in front of a capacity crowd.

"Awe-some!" he breathed. Suddenly, the public address system blared out a deafening test message while images of the World Cup trophy flashed across the giant screens at either end of the stadium. When the racket subsided, Max got his interview with the BBC man – right in the middle of the pitch.

"How many people will be here tomorrow, Paul?" he asked.

"Ninety thousand in the stadium," he replied. "Plus another five hundred million watching on television worldwide."

For a moment or two, the five friends stood in silence – taking in what Paul had just said and savouring their players' eye view of the stadium; then it was time to move on.

The television studio was on the fourth floor of the south west corner, but felt almost as familiar as their own living rooms. The Newskids had spent most of the last month watching pundits analysing matches from its famous semicircular desk against the sweeping panorama of the stands. What they hadn't seen was the overhead lighting rig or the five cameras trained on presenter Chris Wilkinson who was busy rehearsing a player profile sequence with the chief producer, Martin Baxter.

"Lenny Dimaggio, England's bad boy made good," announced Wilkinson, timing his words to fit replays of the striker's winning quarterfinal header. "He's chasing his sixth goal of the tournament – and England's place in the final…"

"Hold it there!" interrupted Baxter. "Can we slo-mo that last shot?"

Sensing a break in proceedings, Paul took the opportunity of making the introductions.

"Excuse me, gentlemen. I'd like you to meet Max, Becky, Ollie, Rachael and Akbar. They're our guests for tomorrow's semifinal."

"You're Newskids on the Net, aren't you?" smiled

Chris Wilkinson, standing to greet them. "I'll make sure to give you a mention on the air."

"And we'll get a shot of you during the build-up," promised Martin Baxter. "You deserve a lot of credit for finding that missing girl. Enjoy the match!"

In spite of his hectic schedule, Chris insisted on having his photograph taken with the kids, then signed autographs for everyone and escorted them back to the lift.

"What a lovely guy!" said Becky when they got back to the TV compound. "Thanks for a brilliant tour, Paul. It was quality!"

But Paul had one final surprise up his sleeve.

"Are there any James Bond fans here?" he asked, pausing outside a shabby truck with *'QUEN'S DEN'* stencilled across the door. The children looked puzzled, but he quickly explained the reason for his question. "The BBC has it own gadget man. His name is Charles Quentin, but everyone calls him 'Q'. He'd find a way of putting a camera on the end of a flying bullet if it would make a programme more exciting."

At the press of a button, the hydraulic door hissed opened and the children squeezed into a space crammed with dismantled cameras, oscilloscopes and TV monitors where a small man, wearing black horn-rimmed glasses held together with pieces of sticky tape, was crawling around on all fours.

"Ah! There you are, you little devil!" he muttered, scrambling to his feet and holding out an object no bigger than a shirt button in the palm of his hand.

Sparks leaned forward for a closer look.

"What's that?" he asked.

"It's my latest contribution to sports broadcasting," replied Charles Quentin. "I call it The Ref Cam. It transmits perfect pictures and sound over a range of three quarters of a mile. The referee has agreed to wear one tomorrow, so we'll be able to replay any controversial incidents from his point of view."

"Wicked!" exclaimed Ollie, "I wish I had one of those! Goston Under 15s get some terrible referees!"

"Then perhaps it's time they were put to the test!" smiled the genial technician. "I've got several prototypes. You're welcome to borrow one for a week or so, if you like."

Ollie couldn't believe his luck as Charles handed over one of the tiny silver buttons and took a miniature radio receiver from an untidy drawer.

"Just plug this receiver into your camera," he explained, "And it will pick up the action from wherever your referee happens to be."

"Thanks a lot, Mr. Quentin!" said Ollie, "I promise you'll get it back!"

"Oh, I'm sure I can trust you!" he laughed with an airy wave of the hand, "And I hope Goston Under 15s get some better decisions in future!"

There was so much more the Newskids wanted to ask about this man's extraordinary world, but it was time to head back to the limo. Ollie and Sparks couldn't wait to try out the Ref Cam and John the driver made a perfect guinea pig. Rachael kept him talking while Sparks stuck the tiny self-adhesive device to the volume control of the stereo and everyone piled inside. The entire journey back to the hotel was spent huddled round the viewfinder of

Ollie's camera, stifling giggles as their hapless chauffeur talked to his girlfriend on a hands-free phone, trying to explain how the phone number of a woman in Godalming had found its way into the top pocket of his best suit.

It was eight thirty when they arrived. The receptionist was just going off duty, but spotted Becky making her way to the lifts and dashed over to her.

"Excuse me, Miss Roberts. There's a message for you."

Becky thanked her and thumbed open the tiny envelope.

"What is it?" asked Max. "Nothing wrong at home, I hope?"

"I think you'd b..better…read this." she faltered, handing him the tightly folded note.

Max went as white as a sheet as he studied three lines of almost illegible scrawl.

Dimaggio's going to lose tomorrow. Meet me 9.30. Fast food trailer five minutes north on A4005. I'll be wearing a red Chicago Bears baseball cap. Say nothing. I'm risking my life.

His brow darkened as he replaced the note in its envelope and turned to the others.

"Becky and I won't be joining you for supper," he said. "I want you three to promise not to let one another out of your sight and, if we're not back by ten thirty, show this message to the police. Unless it's some kind of a hoax, we may be in terrible danger."

Chapter 18

RENDEZVOUS WITH A STRANGER

The illuminated Wembley arch crowned the darkening London skyline as a black cab dropped Max and Becky at a dreary kebab trailer where two Turks were trying to keep up with the orders being shouted at them by an army of fans. The pair felt vulnerable and scared as the driver sped away into the night. They were alone now, cut off from everyone who knew them – except the mysterious owner of a red Chicago Bears baseball cap.

"This is going to be like looking for a needle in a haystack," said Max, eyeing the mass of England and German supporters lying out across the verge. "They're nearly all wearing caps. It'll be best to split up. I'll take the trailer, you take the grass!"

It was almost impossible to tell one colour from another in the failing light. Becky began to pick her way through a maze of outstretched legs, starting as she stumbled over a German who glowered at her, brushing spilt lager from his jeans. She knew that they were playing with fire and a constant stream of questions was running through her head. Which of these faces would turn out to be their contact? What did they want of her? When would they make their move?

It was almost dark when one of the Turks emerged from the caravan to change a gas cylinder. The light from the open doorway cast a fluorescent glow onto a nearby litter bin where Becky could faintly discern the tip of a red cap protruding above the overflowing deposits of drink cans and food wrappers. Heart pounding, she walked forward and peeped over the top. Below her was a crouching figure, hands clasped to the knees, back pressed hard against the side of the bin, rocking anxiously to and fro.She looked around for Max, but he was lost in the crowd.

"E..excuse me…" she said softly.

The figure looked up in alarm. The eyes were hidden behind dark glasses, the face shielded by a baseball cap with a distinctive letter ***C*** across its peak.

"I'm B..Becky Roberts…You left a message for me, I think."

The stranger motioned her to sit and Becky dropped to her knees. Slowly, the glasses came away revealing a pair of delicate blue eyes; then a cascade of auburn hair tumbled onto the shoulders of an attractive woman in her mid-twenties as the cap was removed. Her face was strangely familiar and Becky was trying to remember where she had seen it before. Her mind raced back to the spring evening when Rachael had burst into the shed with her copy of *At Home With The Stars*; she pictured the smiling couple with their two beautiful children and cute Labrador pups – then realised with a shock that she was looking at Terri Dimaggio.

"There you are!" shouted a male voice. "I've been looking everywhere..."

Mrs. Dimaggio covered her face and cowered against the bin, but Becky touched her shoulder with a reassuring hand.

"There's nothing to worry about, Mrs. Dimaggio. This is Max Taylor. He's my best friend. You can trust him."

Max knelt beside them as the woman fumbled in the pockets of her leather jacket for a packet of cigarettes. As the lighter flared, they could see fear etched into her lovely face; then the flame died and she began to speak.

"He's got to be stopped," she said. "Sure, my husband's a national hero and earns the sort of money most people only dream about; but the football pay is nothing compared to the fortune he makes from drugs..."

She hesitated as a drunken fan tossed an empty beer can into the bin and stumbled on his way.

"It started small," she continued quickly, "Selling ecstasy tablets while he was still at school; now he's set his sights on building one of the biggest cocaine and heroin rackets in the world. If everything works out, he won't need to play football in a year's time but, until then, he has to pay a network of dealers and traffickers *and* keep up the superstar lifestyle."

"And that's why he fixes match results..." interjected Becky.

"Shhh! Keep your voice down!" hissed Terri

Dimaggio, her eyes constantly searching for any sign of danger. "If they see me, I'm dead."

"If *who* sees you, Mrs. Dimaggio?" asked Max. "What are you afraid of?"

"There's a gambling syndicate controlled by a man called Reginald Smith," she whispered. "If Lenny produces the right results, it makes millions – and my old man gets the lion's share. If England lose to Germany tomorrow, it'll be the biggest pay day of his life – and he's going to make sure they do."

"But why are you t..telling us this?" asked Becky.

"Because I've nowhere else to turn." Her hand trembled as she raised the cigarette to her lips. "There's no love in our marriage. If I go to the authorities, Len will easily find out and have me killed; but he knows that Newskids on the Net already knows more than is good for him – and that you have links to the BBC. I think you kids may have the best chance of putting a stop to all this."

"But we haven't any *proof*," said Max. "No-one is going to pull an England striker out of a World Cup semifinal on the say-so of a bunch of kids."

"There might be a chance of *getting* your proof," she said, drawing them closer. "That's why I asked you to meet me here. The syndicate is placing massive bets on *how* Germany will win the match, but Smith won't decide what he wants Lenny to do until he knows the half-time score."

"How will Lenny be told?" asked Max, knitting his brow as he considered the facts.

"He'll be given the word in the tunnel, just before the teams go out for the second half. They've set up some phoney photo agency called *Corner Pix* and someone posing as a photographer will brief him while he pretends to take shots. If you can persuade someone to witness *that* conversation, you'll have the evidence that could save thousands of kids from drug dependency *and* England's chances in the World Cup."

The children said nothing as Mrs. Dimaggio threw away her cigarette and replaced the sunglasses and baseball cap. They were still taking in the awesome significance of what they were being asked to do. Suddenly, a coach pulled into the lay-by and dozens more fans spilled onto the grass, clinking bottles and singing at the tops of their voices.

"We can't stay here," she said. "Please promise you'11 do what you can."

Max turned to Becky who nodded her consent.

"Alright, Mrs. Dimaggio," he agreed. "We promise."

The trio clambered to their feet and pushed towards the main road where Max managed to hail a taxi.

"Grand Hotel, please!" he requested as the driver lowered his window.

The teenagers scrambled aboard, but when they looked back, Mrs. Dimaggio had vanished in the crowd.

★★★

London was basking in a heat wave. Temperatures were in the high twenties and,with less than three hours to kick-off, final preparations were in full swing for a match that had already reserved its place in the annals of world football.

A huge responsibility now rested on the shoulders of the five children from Goston and Max had been awake most of the night wondering how best to convince the BBC of Terri Dimaggio's story. He knew that Paul Cooper and his team would be under pressure and they would only get one chance to put their message across; he also knew that they would have to do it before the broadcast began. As the limo approached the stadium, he had prepared a speech and was mentally rehearsing it again and again; but there was an expected snag: a security cordon had been placed round the television compound while police with sniffer dogs checked the area for explosives. By the time anyone was allowed near Paul's trailer, the outside broadcast was live on the air and Max had to go in by himself. The atmosphere was crackling with excitement and, as his eyes adjusted to the dim light, he could see the young producer working flat out – scanning banks of monitors and speaking to a constant stream of voices that blared at him from the control desk.

"Newsroom in London calling Wembley O.B." said one. "*Can you hear me?"*

"Hello, Newsroom. This is Paul at Wembley. How can we help?"

"The Editor wants a two-way with Chris Wilkinson for the one o'clock bulletin."

"No problem. Who'll be interviewing him?"

"Greg Armstrong...and we'll need a scene-set. Can you send us pictures on the link in the next ten minutes?"

Paul turned to his director who was busily feeding a live sequence into daytime television.

"News needs a scene-set in the next ten minutes," he said. "Can you cope?"

The director gave a cursory thumbs up and carried on working. Max knew that this broadcasting rollercoaster was unstoppable. His only option was to interrupt.

"I have something to tell you, Paul!" he called as loudly as he dared. "This is really important!"

The harassed producer turned in surprise and Max was about to say his piece when another voice boomed from the loudspeaker.

"Park Lane Outside Broadcast calling Wembley!"

"Come in, Park Lane."

"The England squad is just leaving the hotel."

Paul looked at the preview monitor which was showing live pictures of a huge crowd cheering the players as they boarded the coach that would take them to the stadium.

"I can't stop now, Max," he said, turning towards him. "I hope you have a great day and don't forget to collect a photographer's pass from the Press Room if Ollie wants to use his camera." Then he swung back into action. "Take Park Lane O.B.!"

Max felt sick to his stomach as the director cut to a close-up of Lenny Dimaggio giving the thumbs up to a group of ten-year-olds, all waving flags of St. George. There was no more time for politeness; he *had* to make someone listen before it was too late.

"Lenny Dimaggio is being paid a fortune to lose this semifinal!" he shouted at the top of his voice.

Heads turned, but only for a moment. As the England coach pulled away, the production team carried on, dismissing the outburst as a rant from a deluded and excitable teenager. Max tried again, but Paul silenced him, spinning impatiently in his swivel chair.

"I don't want to be rude, Max," he said curtly. "But three hours before the start of a World Cup semifinal is no time for BBC Sport to be accusing an England striker of match fixing. Where's your proof?'

"Er...there's nothing concrete...yet..." said Max, trying to hold his nerve. "But if you could just send someone down to the tunnel at half time..."

"Are we making a television programme or not?" called the irate director. "Germany's on the move!"

"You'll have to go now, Max," said Paul, putting a hand firmly on his shoulder and steering him towards the door. "If you can produce some hard evidence, I'll be the first to listen; but right now there are twenty million British football fans waiting for us to provide some first rate coverage and I'd like to get on with the job."

Max felt utterly defeated as the electronic doors closed behind him.

"They wouldn't listen," he said flatly, rejoining the others. "We may as well get Ollie's photographer's pass."

★★★

It was bedlam in the Press Room. With two hours to kick-off, journalists from all over the world were busy filing stories by laptop and mobile phone. Ollie had joined a queue of photographers waiting by a trestle table for a pompous official to issue orange plastic bibs. Each one was marked *PHOTOGRAPHER* and carried a number allocated to a specific newspaper or magazine.

"We're going to roast in these!" complained a man carrying a tripod and three heavy camera bags. Can't I just wear a little badge?"

"What paper are you from?" asked the steward whose sense of humour had long since deserted him.

"The Daily Star."

The bib man scanned his clipboard.

"Daily Star…Daily Star…" he muttered. "That's number 197." Then he riffled through the pile, pulled bib 197 out by its waist tapes and ticked it off the list.

"Next…!"

Max was intrigued by this rather eccentric security ritual and tried to distract himself from Dimaggio by watching the photographers coming and going from the table. Soon, he was staring hard at the diminishing pile of orange tabards as though, somewhere within it, lay the solution to their problem. Suddenly, a fantastic idea came to him.

"I've got it!" he cried, turning to Becky. "Mrs. Dimaggio told us that Lenny was going to get his instructions from someone masquerading as a photographer from some bogus press agency, didn't she?'

"Yes. *Corner Pix.*"

"Well, let's hope he hasn't collected his bib yet."

"Why?"

Max ignored the question and turned excitedly to Sparks.

"Have you got the Ref Cam with you?"

Sparks nodded, then Max revealed his plan.

"No-one would notice a tiny bug the size of a shirt button on a tatty photographer's tabard. If we could attach it to the *Corner Pix* bib, we'd be able to record Dimaggio being told *how* to throw the match; then they'd *have* to believe us."

Becky glanced towards the officious steward who was taking great delight in telling a photographer from *Paris Match* that he wasn't on his list.

"But that p..pompous jobsworth will never let us get close enough to plant a bug," she sighed. "Anyway, how would we know which bib to stick it on?"

As they grappled with the problem, Rachael's eyes remained fixed on the activity around the trestle table. Ollie was next in the queue and she knew that now was the time to act.

"Leave the bib man to me!" she said, fluffing up her hair and slinking over to the steward who was searching his list for *Newskids on the Net.* "Sorry to cut in, honey," she purred, turning on all her American charm. "This is quite a security system you have here. I wonder if you might be able to help me?"

"I'll do my best." said the bib man who had spent most of his morning staring at a procession of unsmiling men and welcomed the attention of an attractive young woman.

"I'm supposed to be meeting a photographer friend, but I can't find him any place. Could you maybe tell me if *Corner Pix* has checked in?"

"It's slightly irregular," he replied, flattered by the attention. "But we aim to please."

"What's going on?" mouthed a bewildered Ollie as the man ran a stubby finger down the list. Rachael tapped her nose knowingly and looked towards Sparks who showed her the Ref Cam ready in his open palm.

"Here we are, miss," said the steward, looking up from the clipboard. "*Corner Pix*. Number 209. Not arrived yet. The bib's still here."

That was exactly what Rachael wanted to hear and it was time to raise the curtain on act two of her plan.

"Oh, no!" she shrieked, dropping her shoulder bag and making sure that the contents scattered as widely as possible across the floor. "My mom always said I fell out of the clumsy tree! Would you mind giving me a hand?"

The man dropped chivalrously to his knees and, in the time it took them to repack the bag, Sparks had found the *Corner Pix* bib and tacked the Ref Cam neatly in place. The trap was set – and half-time would tell whether or not it would snare Lenny Dimmagio once and for all.

Chapter 19

THE JOURNEY OF BIB 209

With thirty minutes to kick-off, every corridor and stairway in the stadium was alive with spectators hurrying to their seats like a colony of ants. The Newskids were wide-eyed at the kaleidoscope of colour and sound that confronted them in the arena.The stands were ablaze with red and white as England fans, some with dyed hair, others with painted faces, waved flags and banners in salute to their heroes who were warming up on the sun-baked pitch; then a flurry of red, yellow and black lifted the German players who sprinted to the opposite end of the field, working every muscle like gladiators in the Colosseum.

Max and the team were sitting in the front row of block G, twenty yards from the tunnel and close to the dugouts from which the managers would soon be trying to spur their teams to victory. If only they knew that the outcome of this historic clash of two great footballing nations was in the hands of five kids from a little town called Goston.

As the players began to leave the field, Ollie was listening in to the Ref Cam on his tiny ear-piece, but could hear only the muffled babble of journalists leaving the Press Room.

"Maybe they're on to us," he sighed, glancing at the photographers fixing long lenses to their cameras in the designated positions around the pitch. "I'll bet Dimaggio's man has been warned off..." Suddenly, he grabbed Max's arm as a sharp crackle told him that, at last, bib 209 was being pulled from the pile. Everyone leaned towards the little viewfinder as a picture of the steward's ample stomach swept onto the screen.

"This is a tunnel pass," he was saying to an unseen photographer. "*The players will be coming out for the national anthems soon. If you don't get a move on, you'll miss your shots."*

Max pressed closer, but the picture turned turtle as the unknown press man tossed the bib over his head and dashed from the room, tying the waist tapes as he ran. The Ref Cam flew along corridors, sending back crystal clear pictures of late-comers scattering in all directions while a burly forearm lashed out at anyone too slow to get out of the way.

"They ought to enter this guy for the Grand National!" cried Sparks as bib 209 shot into an empty lift.

For a moment, the tiny camera lingered on a panel of buttons, then Ollie's blood froze as he watched a long forefinger pressing for level three. It was circled with a tattoo he had hoped never to see again: a coiled snake.

"That's one of the kidnappers!' he gasped as the lift doors closed. "The one called Snake!"

Max didn't answer. He was intent on following the camera's journey along a corridor lined with spectators wearing expensive suits and designer dresses.

"Why is he going to the third floor instead of down to the pitch?" he murmured.

Suddenly, the picture settled on a door marked *PRIVATE – HOSPITALITY ROOM 303* and Ollie pressed the 'record' button as Snake's fist rapped out a sequence of coded knocks.

"Ugh!" shuddered Rachael, staring at the tight, elaborately patterned shirt that clung to the man's muscular forearms like a second skin. "Where does this guy buy his clothes? That sort of stuff went out with the ark!"

The door opened and the craggy face of Reginald Smith filled the screen.

"You're late," he barked as the Ref Cam lurched into a room packed with sleazy, unsmiling men hunched over laptops and talking aggressively into mobile phones; then came the strange, sibilant voice that was terrifyingly familiar.

"Sorry, boss. Traffic round here's at a standstill..."

"The hell with your excuses, Snake!" cursed Smith, glancing at his Rolex. "Get down to the tunnel and start taking pictures. We need to get the marshals used to seeing your ugly mug around. I don't want anyone asking questions when it's time to pass Len the word at half-time."

"What's the situation?"

"We need a nil-nil score line at the break, so I've told him to keep the lid on it. If England come on too strong, he'll play to keep us occupied in defence."

"How do I collect his instructions?"

"I'll call you on the mobile just after the half-time whistle. It'll be noisy down there, so be alert. Your life won't be worth living if you foul things up!"

With seven minutes to kick-off, the stadium was pulsating to the sound of chanting fans; but the Newskids were oblivious to everything but the journey of the Ref Cam. They watched it arrive in the tunnel and move slowly past the England squad – jaws set, mouths tense, boots scuffing at the ground as they waited for the signal to take the field. Suddenly, Dimaggio's face appeared, shooting Snake a furious glance as he pretended to take photographs; then bib 209 swung towards the tunnel mouth where an official was waving the players out onto the pitch. There was a deafening roar as both teams processed into the arena, the Ref Cam following a short distance behind transmitting breathtaking pictures of ninety thousand spectators in a frenzy of anticipation.

For a moment, Ollie took his eyes away from the screen and focused on the tunnel mouth. He was hoping that seeing Snake in the flesh might dispel the nightmarish images that had haunted him for so many months. Suddenly, bib 209 emerged into the sunlight and there he was – every bit as tall and muscular as he remembered, but Rachael had been wrong about the figure-hugging shirt. Snake was wearing a sleeveless vest that displayed an upper body completely tattooed with the exotic markings of a reticulated python.

"I don't like this!" shuddered Sparks. "We've got our evidence now. I vote we hand it straight over to the BBC!"

"Not until half-time!" insisted Max. "We *must* have a confession from Dimaggio himself or they may not accept our story. Please trust me, Sparks. We've got to hold our nerve."

To a fresh crescendo of sound, the match got underway. From the opening whistle,England looked the stronger side – but nevertheless the Newskids watched Dimaggio like hawks. It was soon clear that, while putting on an heroic, almost theatrical performance in attack, he was cunningly ensuring that whenever his fellow forwards had the German defence under pressure, a series of misplaced passes confounded their efforts.

With five minutes to half-time there was still no score and Smith's plan seemed perfectly on track until England broke through again. The crowd roared as the ball found Dimaggio whose strike was, unsurprisingly, aimed wide of the goal; but it glanced off the shoulder of a German defender and rebounded to England captain Steve Betchley who volleyed straight into the back of the net. Tens of thousands of England supporters rose in an ecstasy of joy and the strains of 'Rule Britannia' rocked the stadium until the referee blew for the end of the first half.

As the players left the field, the Newskids saw Snake lurking in the tunnel mouth. Ollie made sure that the camera was recording and they waited for his mobile to ring; but ten minutes later, Smith still hadn't made contact.

"What's going on?" murmured Max. "If he leaves it much longer, it'll be too late."

The P.A. system was encouraging spectators back to

their seats when the call finally came. The last minute goal had clearly caused problems for the occupants of Hospitality Room 303 and Snake looked tense as he received his instructions. Seconds later, the Ref Cam entered the tunnel again, weaving its way past groups of England and German players and officials assembling for the second half. Slowly, it homed in on Dimaggio who had isolated himself from his team-mates and was pretending to tighten a lace. The Newskids were on tenterhooks – and it was Max's turn to listen in.

"It's not lookin' good," Snake was saying as the England striker straightened up. *"That goal's cost us a fortune."*

"It ain't my fault, I was aiming to miss. How was I to know that Betchley would get a lucky deflection off that blond geezer?"

Dimaggio's shifty eyes swept the tunnel, but they were blind to the five teenagers capturing every single word on an amateur video camera.

"Forget about it, Len. Just make sure they equalise…and do it as quick as you can…"

"How do I give 'em the winner?'

The Newskids held their breath. This was the proof for which they had suffered so much.

"The big money's on England losing on a penalty. Smith wants you to give one away…but leave it as late as you can."

"Got it…."

Moments later, the players were lining up for the second half – but the Newskids were under more pressure than anyone on the field. They had their evidence now, and it only remained to show it to someone with the authority to take action before it was too late. The TV compound looked deserted as they raced down the staircase to basement level one. The BBC team was hard at work in the trucks, beaming the drama round the world while uniformed guards patrolled the security barriers.

"Sorry, kids," said one. "Broadcast personnel only beyond this point."

"But we *must* see Paul Cooper," pleaded Max as a huge roar heralded the resumption of play. "We have information about criminal activity that's going to affect the outcome of this match."

"I'm sure you have," said the man, not taking him seriously and completely ignoring Ollie who was trying to play back the recording. "But my instructions are that the TV and Radio teams are not to be disturbed. Why don't you kids go back inside? You're missing some great football."

An aching numbness swept over them as they turned away and headed back to the stadium. It beggared belief that all the justification anyone could need for stopping the match was sitting in Ollie's camera, yet *still* no-one would listen. Max felt wretched as he stood at the back of block G, staring down at their empty seats and wondering how he could bring himself to watch the rest of the game.

Suddenly, there was a gasp from the crowd. A German midfielder had lofted a long ball into the England penalty area and Dimaggio saw a chance to put the opposition back on terms. Sprinting towards the goalmouth, he defeated two forwards then faked a stumble that released the ball to Carl Hassler who rifled it into the top right hand corner of the England net. It was one all!

Max pictured the jubilation in Hospitality Room 303, then a red mist descended and Becky saw that familiar steely glint appear in his eyes.

"I can't just sit back and watch this!" he shouted. "I'm going to the dugout!"

"Oh, no you're not!" shouted Ollie, brandishing the camera. "We're *all* going to the dugout! Right behind you, Max!"

The five friends flew down the aisle, leaped the security barrier at the front of the stand and panted up to the England dugout where the manager, Ted Burgess, was locked in discussion with his coaching team; but he had a match to win – and it wouldn't be easy to get his attention.

"I know this isn't the greatest timing in the world, Mr. Burgess," shouted Max, trying to make himself heard over the cheering German fans. "But we *must* speak to you!"

The marshals were almost upon them now, but Burgess wouldn't listen.

"Dimaggio's a traitor!" yelled Ollie, showing his camera. "We've got evidence here to prove it..."

But he was out of time. Two burly officials grabbed his arms while three more went for Becky, Rachael and Sparks who were darting around like minnows in a desperate effort to divert attention from Max; but it was all in vain. The Newskids were swiftly frogmarched from the arena and Dimaggio was on course to put England out of the tournament.

"You *must* let us go!" pleaded Max as the marshal

herded them into an empty dressing room. "Lenny Dimaggio is a crook. He's being paid a fortune to lose this match. We've got the proof on camera – just look at the recording if you don't believe us."

"I'm not falling for that!' interrupted the man, folding his arms across his chest and sitting heavily in a chair by the door. "And I'm not letting you lot out of my sight until I'm satisfied that you're ready to behave like civilised human beings. Now shut up and put that thing away!"

The next fifteen minutes were sheer torture. Their stomachs churned harder with each roar of the crowd until Max could bear it no longer. Enough was enough!

"Excuse me, sir," he said, launching the biggest charm offensive of his short TVcareer, "Would you mind telling me where the toilets are?"

"Turn right, second door on your left," grunted the marshal, looking up from a dog-eared paperback. "Only you, mind! The rest of you stay where I can see you!"

The cheering swelled as Max opened the door – then he turned on his heel and yelled to the others at the top of his voice.

"Quick! We're out of here! Follow me!"

Before the marshal knew what was happening, they were past him and away down the corridor.

"If we get separated, head for the BBC studio!" panted Max, "It's our last chance!"

As they piled into the lift, the marshal was thirty yards behind – shouting into his walkie-talkie.

"We'll have to move fast," gasped Ollie as the doors closed. "He'll know where we are by the indicator!"

Red lights were flashing above the door as they

arrived at the television studio where two more security men were standing guard.

"Excuse me!" cried Becky, sliding to a breathless halt. "We're Newskids on the Net!"

"I know you are," said the first man. "'My kids watch your show every Wednesday. You should be proud of yourselves for finding that missing girl."

Max felt a surge of relief.

"You've got to help us!" he pleaded, glancing back along the corridor. "We need to talk to Chris Wilkinson. It's a matter of life and death."

"Steady!" said the guard, alarmed at the state he was in. "You'll have a heart attack in a minute! Look, I'd like to help, but I can't let you in now. Chris is covering the World Cup. It will have to wait until they're off air, I'm afraid."

At that moment, the marshal clattered into the corridor with five more men in tow.

"There they are!" he yelled.

The net was closing in, but Max suddenly remembered that there was still one more card left to play.

"Will you do something for us?" he begged, throwing himself at the mercy of the friendly security man. "Just hold the marshals off while I make one phone call. Please! This is really important!"

There was no doubting his sincerity and the man agreed to do as he'd been asked.

"I'll do my best, son," he said, "Go ahead and make your call."

Hands trembling, Max selected a number he had stored in his mobile and pressed 'call'.

"Panic over," said the guard, raising a conciliatory palm to the pack of panting officials. "We'll take over from here."

"But they invaded the pitch!" shouted the angry marshal, "We're under orders to hand them over to the police."

The number still hadn't picked up and Max looked imploringly at his champion as the man's colleagues surrounded his friends.

"Er...I will take personal responsibility for these children," he promised, trying to buy the teenager the time he needed.

"BBC Newsroom." answered a voice.

"Greg Armstrong, please!" said Max assertively. "This is very urgent. Tell him it's Max Taylor from Newskids on the Net."

The line died for a few seconds, then the voice returned.

"Putting you through, Mr. Taylor."

Max smiled with relief and turned gratefully to the security guard.

"I think I've found someone who'll vouch for us," he said, glancing at his watch. There were fifteen minutes left to play as Greg came on the line...

Chapter 20

SETTLING THE SCORE

Moments later, Martin Baxter, the chief producer, appeared. His manner left them in no doubt that their story had been given the very highest priority and, ignoring the commotion in the corridor, he ushered them inside.

"What's the score?" asked Max, fearing that Dimaggio may already have made his move. "Still one apiece," replied Baxter, striding through to the videotape room where editors and statisticians were viewing the match from a dozen different angles. "Where's that footage?"

Ollie handed over the recording and Baxter passed it to his chief engineer.

"I'd like you to play this to the panel," he said. "And be sure to make a copy. It's irreplaceable."

As they moved into the studio, the children saw the vast crowd heaving with excitement through the picture window. Chris Wilkinson raised his hand in greeting, but this was no time for pleasantries. Both teams were fighting to break the one all deadlock and he was already planning the full-time analysis with former England captain, Ryan Schofield and Bill Marsden, the charismatic Chairman of the English Football Association.

"Sorry to butt in, gents," said Baxter, leaning urgently across the desk. "Greg Armstrong has just called. The newsroom wants us to look at some material these kids shot at half-time. If it's genuine, it will headline all today's bulletins and could change the course of the match."

"Ready to roll!" hummed a voice from the intercom.

The children felt their stomachs tingle as the BBC team turned its attention to the studio monitor where, unseen by the viewing millions, their recording appeared. The players and officials milling in the tunnel mouth proved that the material had been recorded at half-time and brows darkened as the Ref Cam homed in on Lenny Dimaggio.

"How do I give 'em the winner?"

"The big money's on England losing on a penalty. Smith wants you to give one away. But leave it as late as you can."

"Got it..."

Producer and panellists gasped in disbelief, but the evidence spoke for itself and they were faced with the stark reality that the man expected to win the game for England was a cheat and a crook.

"There's no time to ask how you managed to get this footage, kids," said Marsden. "But it's genuine alright. We've got to get Dimaggio off the field."

"How are we going to do that?" asked Wilkinson. "If Ted Burgess pulls off his star striker ten minutes from the end of a World Cup semifinal drawn at one all there'll be a riot!"

The words had scarcely passed his lips than the crowd rose in alarm. The England goal was under threat. Desperate cries of 'Clear it! Get rid of it!' soared into the air as a German midfielder moved into position for a strike. This was the chance Dimaggio had been waiting for and he launched himself into a vicious sliding tackle that catapulted the player into the air and sent him sprawling on his back. The crowd gasped as an ear-splitting whistle halted play. With a phoney display of remorse, the striker helped his winded opponent to his feet; but the foul had to be punished and Germany was set to take the lead – on a penalty.

"I can't sit back and watch this!" snapped Bill Marsden in disgust as England retreated behind the box. But he was powerless to act. Goalkeeper Mike Farley was already preparing to face Hans Lieberman's kick.

The crowd fell silent as the powerful German paced back from the ball, then stood motionless, placing every ounce of concentration on the single shot that would almost certainly put England out of the tournament.

Farley braced himself, muscles tense, brain alert, weighing every nuance of a decision he would have less than a split second to take. Should he dive left? Would it curl right? Should he jump high? Would it go low? With a dull thud, the German's boot connected with the ball which seemed to fly in slow motion towards the goalmouth. The England keeper launched himself towards the centre of the left hand post where both gloves met the ball with a smack that echoed through the stadium like a rifle shot.The stands erupted and the German sank to his knees in anguish. England had held the match at one all!

Back in the studio, Bill Marsden flung his jacket over the back of a chair and made for the door.

"If Burgess will listen to anyone, he'll listen to me," he called. "I'm going to the dugout and I want you kids to come with me. Bring your camera! We'll need to play him that film!"

Taking the stairs three at a time, Marsden led the dash to the back of the lower north stand. Marshals and spectators were dumbfounded to see the Chairman of the Football Association sprinting down the aisle and leaping the security barrier with the Newskids hard on his heels.

The England manager was discussing a substitution with his assistant coach when he saw them coming. Ted Burgess knew that only something of the utmost importance would have brought Bill Marsden to the touchline, but any interruption was unwelcome at such a critical point in the match.

"Can't this wait, Bill?" he snapped as the group arrived at the dugout. "We're seven minutes from time. I've got a game to win!"

"Thirty seconds is all I ask!" panted Marsden.

Burgess eyed him with concern.

"I'm listening," he said. "You've got ten!"

"Dimaggio's stitching you up! He gave away that penalty because he's on a massive back-hander from an international gambling syndicate.You've got to pull him off or he's going to try again!"

Burgess stared in disbelief. If he had been hearing

this from anyone other than the Chairman of English Football's governing body he would have had them escorted from the pitch.

"How do you know this?" he asked, sinking onto the bench as he faced the most crucial decision of his career. "The whole country's pinning its hopes on Lenny winning this for England. What if he's innocent? There'll be mayhem if I pull him off!"

"But he's *not* playing to win for England!" blurted Max, unable to contain himself as another Dimaggio strike flashed wide of the post. "He's playing to win for Germany!"

"The lad's right, Ted," panted Marsden. "Watch this. It was recorded in the tunnel at half-time."

Burgess looked grim as he watched the footage on Ollie's tiny screen. Having seen the evidence for himself, he sprang to his feet and turned to a young player wearing number twenty on his shirt.

"No time for a warm-up, Jimmy. You're going on for Len."

"What?" said the player in amazement. "*Me*...for *Len*...but *why*...?"

"Because I say so!" barked the boss, rounding on his assistant. "I want Dimaggio off! Twenty for Nine! Show the board!"

There was uproar as the substitution board was raised. Tens of thousands of England fans voiced their disapproval as Dimaggio left the field, his face contorted with rage as he headed for the England dugout. Amid the confusion, a man ran onto the pitch to intercept him. He was wearing an orange bib and carrying a camera. Max recognised him instantly. It was Snake.

"Quick, Ollie! Start recording again!" he shouted as the two men made contact off the pitch. "This isn't over yet!"

Ollie pressed the red button and inserted his tiny ear-piece. The Ref Cam was still working and Snake's voice came through loud and clear.

"The kids have grassed you up!" he was yelling, pretending to take pictures. "The fat one's just shown Burgess something on that naffin' camera of his!" Dimaggio's eyes narrowed as he took in the situation in the dugout.

"Get the chopper here fast!" he barked. "If they've rumbled me, I'll make for the roof. Tell the boys to airlift me out from there!"

Suddenly, Snake's camera appeared to fail. Ollie saw him open the back and slip something into the palm of his hand.

"I think you might need this, Len," he said, passing it to the striker as he ran from touchline.

Arriving at the dugout, Dimaggio squared up to the England manager. "You're finished in football, Burgess!" he snarled. "They'll never forgive you!"

The home supporters knew that Dimaggio's substitution had given Germany the psychological advantage and the booing in the stadium had reached a massive crescendo; but suddenly, a familiar voice thundered from the P.A. system and the angry hubbub began to subside.

"Ladies and gentlemen, the match is being suspended for an important announcement. May we please draw your attention to the screens at either end of the stadium?"

There was a murmur of surprise from the England fans as they recognised Chris Wilkinson speaking live from the BBC studio.

"There is no cause for alarm," he said. "This will only take a moment."

A hush fell as twenty-two players, ninety thousand spectators and a worldwide television audience waited to hear what the presenter had to say.

"Evidence has come to light that, from the very beginning of this match, things have not been quite as they appeared. A decision has been taken at the highest level that, in the interests of a great tournament that has so far been played in the spirit of peace and fair play, this evidence should be made public without delay." A wave of disquiet spread through the stands as Wilkinson prepared to drop one of the greatest bombshells in sporting history. "Most of you are wondering why Lenny Dimaggio has been removed from the field. We have a recording that answers that question. It was made in the tunnel during the half-time interval by a group of teenagers who call themselves Newskids on the Net."

The shot of Chris Wilkinson dissolved to Ollie's recording and everyone watched in silence as Dimaggio's face filled the two huge screens.

"How do I give 'em the winner?"

"The big money's on England losing on a penalty. Smith wants you to give one away. But leave it as late as you can."

"Got it..."

The footage raised gasps of disbelief in homes, stadiums, pubs and clubs throughout the world. At Wembley, slow handclapping broke out in the north stand, quickly spreading to the east, then to the west until the entire complex was shaking with a deafening outpouring of anger and disgust.

Dimaggio's eyes blazed with fury as the spectre of international disgrace stared him in the face. He had nothing to lose now and would go to any lengths to save his own skin.

"Stay back!" he warned, producing a small revolver from his fist. As the England support team shrank back, Ollie realised that the weapon had been hidden inside Snake's camera – but it was now pointing squarely at Max. Becky screamed as Dimaggio grabbed her best friend by the neck and dragged him towards the tunnel. Shouts from the stand quickly alerted the police to the firearm glinting against the teenager's head and an officer rushed forward, his helmet tumbling to the ground as he closed on the striker.

"Please remain calm, ladies and gentlemen," appealed another voice from the tannoy.

Suddenly, two shots rang out and the shouts turned to screams as the policeman slumped to the ground, bleeding heavily from the chest and neck. Spectators fled in panic and a team of paramedics raced to his aid while the Newskids stood helplessly by, watching Dimaggio retreat into the tunnel using Max as a human shield.

"We've sealed all exits," announced Commander Brian Newby of the Metropolitan Police, arriving at the dugout with three senior officers. "Does anyone know the name of the young hostage?"

"His name's M..Max T…Taylor," sobbed Becky. "He's going to be killed, I know he is! That pig has already shot a policeman. What has he got to lose?"

"Try to keep calm, miss. We're doing everything we can." reassured the police chief turning to Ted Burgess. "Do you have any idea where Mr. Dimaggio might be going, sir?"

The dazed England coach shook his head, but Ollie knew the answer.

"He's making his way up to the roof," he cried. "They're sending a helicopter to pick him up and, if my guess is right, it'll be coming from Tambleford Aerodrome."

Newby was astounded that a fourteen-year-old should be so well informed and looked to Burgess for confirmation; but the bewildered England coach could only shrug.

"These kids have been right all along," he said. "I'd listen to them if I were you."

By now, Dimaggio had reached the highest tier of the north stand. Keeping a tight grip on Max's shirt, he was manoeuvring him along one of the short passageways leading out to an almost vertical bank of seating. A hum of speculation simmered in the scorching summer air as they inched forward, unnoticed by the wall of spectators – each one mesmerised by the drama unfolding below. Dimaggio glanced down at the pitch where a group of police marksmen was gathering on the touchline. For a moment, Max felt reassured – then gagged as the pressure on his collar tightened he was yanked back into the shadows.

"Time to move on, you little creep!" snarled Dimaggio, retreating along the passage and out onto a deserted walkway. He badly needed a clear space to make his rendezvous with the helicopter, but there were too many openings through which the police could gain access and foil any attempt at an airlift. The pressure of the gun barrel against Max's neck was almost unbearable as they stumbled on; then the big man paused, searching for a way up to a higher position. Max seized the moment to catch his breath but, almost at once, they were on the move again – pushing through a set of swing doors and powering up two flights of stairs towards roof level.

The wind tugged at their hair as they burst into sunlight and the striker, visibly rattled,bent his hostage double over a safety rail as he looked down at the crowds and emergency vehicles massing on the concourse. Max had always been afraid of heights and his stomach was gripped by a violent tingling sensation, as though some invisible force were pulling him over the edge. He looked away, keeping his eyes fixed on the towering arch that seemed more awesome than ever at such close quarters; straddling the stadium like a vast colossus; one massive leg rising only yards from where they stood.

"What are you staring at, wimp?" barked Dimaggio, his head jerking up in alarm as he followed the teenager's gaze towards the world famous symbol of English football.Suddenly, his eyes narrowed as he spotted something inside the arch. It was a gantry from which a two-man maintenance cart ran on overhead rails inside the massive criss-crossed tunnel of steel. "Nobody will get at us four hundred feet up!" he growled. "Come on!"

Max's feet were barely touching the ground as he

was dragged forward again, but Dimaggio stopped in his tracks when he saw that the arch passed several metres wide of the stadium with nothing but a sheer drop between them and the platform.

"There's got to be a way out to that lift!" he raged. "Stay here or so help me I'll shove you over the edge!"

Pushing Max to his knees, he began to heave on a heavy winch handle. For a few moments, nothing seemed to be happening; then a narrow gang-plank began to extend from the side of the building, moving slowly out towards the platform where it locked in place with a metallic clang.

"Get out there!" bawled Dimaggio. "There's a chopper on its way and you're coming with me for insurance!"

The teenager tried not to look down as he was forced along the rickety drawbridge, but the crowd had spotted them now and it was impossible to ignore the sea of upturned faces far below. There was a sudden gasp as, inches from the gantry, Max missed his footing and lurched forward, saving himself by clinging to the safety rail and struggling up onto the platform.

"Get in!" snarled the striker, sending him reeling into the cart with a cruel knee in the back. "Once we're up top, we can sit tight till they pick us up!"

Clambering in after him, the footballer stabbed at a row of buttons until the cart juddered slightly and started upwards with a quiet hum, climbing like a fairground car towards the apex of a gigantic rollercoaster. Max stared at the floor, clinging desperately to his seat as they rose higher and higher until the whole of London was spread beneath them and the pitch looked like a tiny green handkerchief framed by the vast stadium roof.

Becky had seen the cart set off on its journey. She was too far off to identify the occupants, but knew in her heart that one of them was Max. Rachael comforted her as she gazed upwards, her eyes filling with tears.

They were now at the highest point of their ascent and Dimaggio pressed a red button marked 'stop'. The cart slowed to a halt and they were suspended from the very top of the towering structure, with no sound but the rushing wind.

Every camera in the stadium was now trained on the tiny cradle and, for twenty minutes, live pictures were beamed around the world. Back in Goston, Max's parents watched helplessly as their son was held at gunpoint by a desperate criminal while the pupils of Bridgemont School stared in shocked amazement at the television Mr. Aynsley had set up in the hall.

Suddenly, a red helicopter appeared over the horizon, shimmering through the heat haze until its whirring rotor blades hovered forty feet above the cart. A man in a black rescue suit had emerged from the doorway, suspended from a winch. Twisting and swaying, he was guiding himself towards the pair, making sweeping upward movements with both arms. Dimaggio realised immediately that, in order for the man to reach them, they would have to climb out of the cart and onto the surface of the arch itself. Gripping the pistol between his teeth, he heaved himself onto one of the thick, metal tubes, then turned to Max.

"You're coming with me, wimp!" he thundered. "Get out or I'll put a bullet through your interfering little head!"

Max had no choice. Petrified with fear, he swung a leg out of the cart, then froze as the downdraft from the chopper shook it violently. Meanwhile, two armed police officers had stationed themselves on the gantry, but they were unable to open fire for fear of hitting Max or sending the helicopter plummeting into the crowd.

Dimaggio was raging now.

"Let go, damn you!" he screamed, pulling viciously at the schoolboy's wrists and breaking his grip on the safety handle. As Max was pulled out, his foot knocked against the control panel, setting the cradle on its way again; but before he had time to notice, he was clinging desperately to a steel tube, his life passing before him as his legs flailed in space four hundred feet above the stadium.

"Up here! Quick!" screamed the striker, heaving himself onto the outer surface of the arch while the cart continued its downward journey.

Max trembled as he hauled himself up the slippery metal frame until he was close enough for Dimaggio to pull him onto the summit where he crouched on all fours, arms aching from the climb and almost paralysed with fear. Looking up, he could see that the man in black was now only feet away from them, his head encased in a full-face helmet,eyes protected by tinted goggles.

"Strap yourself in and clip on to me!" he shouted

over the roaring rotors, passing a safety harness to Dimaggio who tucked the gun under his chin and began to fasten the webbing straps.

"There's no time for the kid!" he shouted, "Get me into that chopper and let's get out of here!"

As the helicopter took the strain on the line, Max was surprised to see the rescuer turn towards him.

"Hold tight, Max!" he called. "Not much longer now!"

Dimaggio raised his head in alarm.

"How come you know the kid's name?" he roared, pressing the gun into the man's face. "You're Old Bill, aren't you? Tell me the truth or I'll blow your head off!"

Max then realised that his friends had passed on information that enabled the authorities to scramble a helicopter of their own; he also realised that, now Dimaggio knew the truth, the man on the winch was in grave danger. It was then that the feelings of anger and injustice that had been simmering inside him for months reached boiling point. Without a thought for his own safety, he launched himself into space, clutching the flootballer's legs tightly above the knee and biting his thigh as hard as he could. The striker screamed with pain and reached down to ward off the attack; but that one fleeting distraction was all the rescuer needed. As Dimaggio straightened to level the pistol again, the man's helmet smashed into his forehead with sickening force, leaving him hanging like a rag doll.

Max's strength was failing now and the stadium swam below him as he desperately tried to keep his grip on the player's legs. He was faintly aware of the cart reaching the top of the arch and a burly police officer in a blue flak jacket crouching directly below the hovering chopper.

"Jump, Max! Jump!" he called.

Too exhausted to hold on any longer, Max slid into the officer's outstretched arms while the entire stadium erupted in cheers and applause. As the cart began its return journey an unconscious Lenny Dimaggio, the three lions fluttering indignantly on his England shirt, was winched aboard the helicopter and taken into custody.

Meanwhile, Max had collapsed against the officer's chest and was conscious only of a rising crescendo of sound: the cart humming against the wind; anxious voices raised over a clamouring crowd; castors rolling over a bumpy surface; doors banging; footsteps racing; sirens wailing – then silence.

★★★

The figure keeping vigil at his bedside tensed as his eyelids flickered.

"Max! Max! Can you hear me?"

"There are still five minutes to play…" he rambled. "…Get the gun…I'm falling…"

The room swam as he opened his eyes and, through a watery mist, Becky drifted into focus.

"Take it easy!" she said. "You're meant to be resting. The doctor has given you a sedative."

"Where am I?" he asked blearily. "What doctor? What's happening?"

"You're back in the hotel room. You've been asleep for hours."

"What time is it?"

"Nine thirty."

"Where are the others?"

"Here!" called Ollie, moving forward with Rachael and Sparks. "We were told not to excite you, so we've been sitting here very quietly eating your fruit and sampling that Swiss chocolate in the mini-bar!" Then, ruffling his hair, he added: "We're really proud of you, bro! How're you feeling?"

Max nodded. He wanted no reminders of his aerial encounter with Dimaggio, but there was a five hour black hole in his life and he needed to know what he'd missed.

"How's that policeman?" he asked.

"He's off the danger list," said Becky. "They took him to the Central Middlesex. His family's with him now."

"And Dimaggio?"

"Mr. Lenny Dimaggio is facing charges of attempted murder, drug dealing and corruption," smiled Rachael, putting on her best TV presenter voice. "There's going to be a full investigation into his affairs and, thanks to a tip-off from a certain Mr. Sniffer Morris, the police raided Hospitality Room 303 and netted Reginald Smith and quite a few other big time fraudsters."

"And what about the match?"

"Both teams have agreed to replay it tomorrow," said Sparks. "Kick-off's at noon."

A smile of relief and satisfaction spread across Max's face.

"Yesssssss!" he murmured, then the smile faded and he turned to Becky. "Do you think they'll let us stay here and watch or does the stretch limo turn into a pumpkin at midnight?"

"That's out of our hands, I'm afraid," she said. "But one or two people are pulling strings. We might get lucky."

"Who are they?" asked Max, still feeling groggy and confused.

"They're waiting to see you, as it happens," said Ollie, grinning broadly as he opened the door. Max couldn't believe his eyes as into the room trooped Ted Burgess, Terri Dimaggio and the entire England squad.

"Well done, kids," said captain Steve Betchley, handing Max a football signed by every member of the team. "We'll never be able to thank you for what you did today."

"Yes – and now *we've* got it all to do again tomorrow!" joked Mike Farley. "And after I pulled off the best save of my career, too!"

★★★

The following day, the Newskids joined Ted Burgess on the bench for a privileged view of ninety minutes of hard-fought, competitive football. As England made its first attack on the German goal, Max gave Becky's hand a squeeze. She squeezed back and waited for him to pull away – but he didn't. The events of the last twenty-four hours had brought them closer than ever and they were still clinging to each other when England won a place in the final with a classic goal fifteen minutes from time.

★★★

The five kids said very little as the stretch limousine began its journey back to Goston. After their whirlwind three-day adventure, the thought of returning to the real world was something of an anticlimax.

"Double English first period tomorrow," said Ollie gloomily, remembering the essay he had to write that night. "What a come down, eh?"

"Do you want to know something?" asked Max as the great arch sank below the horizon. "When we met Terri Dimaggio, I didn't think we had a hope of pulling this off."

"Do you want to know something else?" said Rachael, whose mind was turning in a rather different direction. "I'm starved. I wish I'd brought enough money to buy the biggest cheeseburger and fries known to man."

The others turned out their pockets, then fell about laughing as they realised that they hadn't got five pounds between them – and there was no more room service in luxury hotels.

"Don't worry. Uncle Sniffer will take care of it!" said Ollie mysteriously, tapping on the glass privacy window. The others eyed each other suspiciously as the driver slid back the partition. "How did I do, John?"

"Not badly at all, Ollie!" he replied, reaching into the glove compartment and passing him a handful of crisp ten pound notes.

"Where did that come from?" asked Max as Ollie gleefully counted out the cash.

"Faith, my dear Max, you must have faith!" he replied, grinning from ear to ear. "I never doubted we'd put Dimaggio in his place. That's why I asked John to bet twenty pounds of my hard-earned pocket money on England to win. Now it's time to share the spoils. Come on, guys. There's a Burger King in the next high street – and I suppose it'll have to be my treat!'